VENGEANCE
OF THE
LAST ROMAN LEGION

BOOK IV

VINDICTA

MARK CARLSON

MILFORD
HOUSE
an imprint of Sunbury Press, Inc.
Mechanicsburg, PA USA

MILFORD HOUSE

an imprint of Sunbury Press, Inc.
Mechanicsburg, PA USA

For information about special discounts for bulk purchases, please contact Sunbury Press Orders Dept. at (855) 338-8359 or orders@sunburypress.com.

To request one of our authors for speaking engagements or book signings, please contact Sunbury Press Publicity Dept. at publicity@sunburypress.com.

FIRST MILFORD HOUSE PRESS EDITION: November 2022

Set in Adobe Garamond Pro | Interior design by Crystal Devine | Cover by Alessandra Smith | Edited by Sarah Peachey.

Publisher's Cataloging-in-Publication Data
Names: Carlson, Mark, author.
Title: Vengeance of the last roman legion: book IV - vindicta / Mark Carlson.
Description: First trade paperback edition. | Mechanicsburg, PA : Milford House Press, 2022.
Summary: In this final chapter of the Vengeance of the last Roman Legion series, the past and present collide in the woods of Germany as Lucius Cassius at last wreaks the revenge he so long sought. A battle of good against evil, of traitors and patriots has taken two thousand years to fulfill the destiny of two nations.
Identifiers: ISBN : 979-8-88819-016-6 (softcover) | 979-8-88819-017-3 (ePub).
Subjects: FICTION / Thrillers / Suspense | FICTION / Thrillers / Terrorism | FICTION / Alternative History | FICTION / Science Fiction / Military.

Product of the United States of America
0 1 1 2 3 5 8 13 21 34 55

Continue the Enlightenment!

This work is dedicated to my late wife, Jane Marie Carlson (1956–2020), who, for twenty-five years, was my love, my friend, and my soulmate. She saw the eagle in me long before I did. She supported my wish to be a writer even when it showed little promise of success. I lost Jane in April 2020, when I was entering the last phase of editing. For months I was certain I could never write again. But she had sacrificed too much for me to give up, and so I sat down to continue the work you are about to read. The eagle has flown. Rest in eternal peace, my beloved.

And to my Lord and Savior, my God saved me when my heart was breaking and showed me the way to peace and happiness. I am forever humbled by God's love and guidance. To God I dedicate my life as a Christian and vow to use the gifts to reach others with the Lord's word.

CONTENTS

TO THE READER

There are four books in this series. Books I, III, and IV take place in the second decade of the twenty-first century, while Book II goes back to the first century AD. With any fiction work there has to be an element of reality. Fiction has to be believable. Even a novel with a nearly impossible plot and storyline must be built on a foundation of credibility. In this work many places, organizations, and technology are real and even familiar to the average twenty-first-century reader. The structure and history of the Roman Empire are based on history, as is that of France, Belgium, and Germany. While I freely admit that the story is completely from my imagination, I would not discount the chance that it could come true.

The geography and flora of northeastern France, Belgium, and west central Germany play a major role in this story. Descriptions have been altered in order to further the credibility of the unfolding drama. While the general terrain, rivers, and mountain ranges exist, the forests and rural areas have been moved or altered to suit the story.

I do not intend to imply that the scenes depicted in these regions are as described, and apologize to the reader for any misunderstanding. For those readers familiar with the history of the Roman Army, you may notice that the legion in the story is numbered LIV, for fifty-four. I realize there was never a fifty-fourth legion. So read on, and enjoy. Remember, this is a work of fiction.

Mark Carlson
San Diego, California Fall 2022

LEGION ORGANIZATION

This book contains several instances where certain specific unit names and ranks are mentioned. In order to avoid confusion, below is a breakdown of how a Roman Legion was organized.

1 Legion: 4,800 men each of

10 Cohorts: 480 men each of

6 Centuries: 80 men each of

10 Contubernium: (tent/mess) 8 men each

COHORTS

Cohort I: Primus

Cohort II: Secundus

Cohort III: Tertius

Cohort IV: Quartus

Cohort V: Quintus

Cohort VI: Sextus

Cohort VII: Septimus

Cohort VIII: Octavus

Cohort IX: Nomus

Cohort X: Decimus

CENTURIES

Each cohort has six centuria in three groups of two.

First Century: Pilus Prior

Second Century: Pilus Posterior

Third Century: Princeps Prior

Fourth Century: Princeps Posterior

Fifth Century: Hastatus Prior

Sixth Century: Hastatus Posterior

Before you embark on a journey of revenge, dig two graves.
—Confucius

Beware the fury of a patient man.
—John Dryden

PROLOGUE

FLIGHT TO OZ

The Gulfstream IV business jet waited outside the guarded NATO hangar at the Brussels airport as the van pulled up near the port wing. The sleek jet was painted a clean blue and white with the four-pointed NATO star on the tall vertical stabilizer. After saying goodbye to the van driver, Alex Braden hopped out and greeted the pilot waiting by the open rear cabin door. "I'm Alex Braden," he said, holding up his NATO credentials. "And you're Captain Dacres?"

The pilot, a slim, dark-haired Frenchman, wore a simple flight suit with his rank badges sewn on the shoulders. "*Oui, monsieur.* Welcome aboard. The plane is fueled and pre-flighted, and the flight plan has been filed. Once you are all aboard, we may take off."

"*Merci*, Captain. Is General Worden already aboard?"

Dacres nodded. "*Oui*, he arrived a short time ago."

"Fine," Braden replied as the ground crew efficiently loaded their luggage onto the jet. "I guess we're ready."

Ready for what? Braden thought. *I can't believe we're doing this.* But it was really happening. He marveled that it had been little more than a week since his bizarre quest had begun.

Alex Braden, an American criminal investigator attached to the North Atlantic Treaty Organization, four companions, and a German Army general were about to fly to Germany for one purpose—to find the last survivors of a lost Roman Legion that had hibernated in a French stone cellar for two thousand years. Legio LIV Vindicta had sealed themselves into the underground lair in the reign of Emperor Augustus. Two weeks before, the surviving soldiers of the long-vanished Roman Empire had emerged from their cellar to find a new world that was both dangerous and incomprehensible. Marching only by night and concealing themselves by day, a thousand legionaries traveled through rural France and Belgium and crossed the Rhine River into Germany. They were out to seek revenge on the descendants of the Germanic tribes that had ambushed and slaughtered more than twenty-four hundred Roman legionaries and civilians in AD 9.

The first clues emerged when Braden learned of the murder of two Belgian state police officers by men using Roman legionary weapons. That was only one of several strange events linked by time and geography from the cellar in France and across three countries. The most serious was the hijacking of a Rhine River towboat and barge by a band of men who wore Roman armor and spoke Latin. Slowly, piece by piece, Braden and his fellow investigators in the Legal Services Department of NATO Headquarters in Brussels uncovered the most bizarre and impossible military invasion in the history of the world.

After eliminating the logical, Braden came to the impossible but inescapable conclusion that living Roman legionaries from the first century had somehow survived and invaded twenty-first-century Germany. With the help of respected British archaeologist Professor Arthur Morley and skilled forensics specialist Doctor Sharon Kelly, Braden gained the support of his superiors at NATO and key members of the German Bundeswehr and government. While an extensive air and ground search along the Romans' route had failed to find or contain them, Doctor Kelly found several dead legionaries in a shallow grave near the Rhine. This finally convinced chronically skeptical German Landespolizei Commissioner Karl Schroeder that the Romans not only existed but presented a deadly threat to a pro-NATO rally being held near the Westerwald, a vast forest in central Germany. The only way to protect the tens of thousands of innocent civilians attending the rally from being attacked by the vengeful Romans was to establish a solid phalanx of armed riot police. But they had to find the Romans first.

For this reason, Braden, Morley, Sharon Kelly, and another NATO investigator, Barney Rabble, were flying to Germany. It had to be the most unusual mission in history. They had set out to find and stop an invasion by men born before Jesus Christ. Shaking his head in wonderment, Braden waved for the others to come over.

His longtime girlfriend, Ann Hamilton, was the first to climb the stairs. Braden asked her to come along for moral support, but her background as an emergency medical technician might also prove useful. Ann's radiant blonde hair shone in the morning sunlight as she smiled at the handsome French pilot. "Lovely day for flying," she said in her crisp English accent.

Dacres tipped his cap to her. "Welcome aboard, mademoiselle," he said. "Please make yourself comfortable."

Ann accepted his hand as she climbed the four steps to the door and ducked inside.

Barney Rabble grinned as he entered the plane. "Next stop, Oz," he said in a voice only Braden heard.

"No kidding," Braden replied, also smiling. Rabble endured constant ribbing over his name but was one of the most brilliant and intuitive investigators at NATO. Braden was sure his skills would be essential when they reached their destination.

Professor Arthur Morley, a sixty-six-year-old archaeologist from Cambridge University, was next. Clad, as always, in khaki slacks and a casual jacket, Morley had thinning gray hair and thick black eyebrows over a florid round face that radiated perpetual good humor. "This should be quite an adventure," he said in his avuncular voice. "I'm actually quite looking forward to it."

"That makes two of us," said Sharon from behind her mentor. "I can't wait to get there." Doctor Sharon Kelly had a long braid of coppery red hair down her back. While Ann had the cameo skin so prized by English women, Sharon's face was tanned and showed the effects of working outdoors on archaeological sites around Europe. Doctor Kelly of Harvard University was now the world's leading expert on the physiology of first-century Roman legionaries. She was eager to find and examine the living Romans, but time was running out.

Braden climbed into the sleek jet last. The cabin was spacious and comfortable, part passenger plane, part flying command center. Besides the rows of plush seats, there was a conference table, computer terminal, fax machine, secure communications system, and a bulkhead-mounted television.

Sharon and Ann sat up front with Morley while Rabble stood by the computer, talking to General Hermann Worden, who turned as Braden entered. "Ah, Herr Braden," Worden said with a wide smile under his closely cropped light brown hair and gray eyes. "We're all here?" The officer, who served as the German Bundeswehr's senior liaison to NATO, was tall, handsome, and stood as straight as if he had swallowed a broom handle. He was dressed in a neat gray field uniform shirt and trousers, polished black shoes, and a peaked cap.

"Yes, General," Braden said, impressed as always with the German officer's strong command presence. "Ready when you are."

Worden turned and walked toward the cockpit, but just then, there was a strident chirping sound. Worden grabbed a radio clipped to his belt. "Forgive me, but I must take this call." Without another word, he went out the cabin door and down the stairs.

Rabble turned to Braden. "That was strange."

"Why?" Braden asked.

Rabble pointed at the array of high-technology communications gear. "He could take a collect call from Mars with all this stuff. Why use a separate radio?"

Braden shrugged. "Maybe it was a personal call."

"Bullshit," Rabble said. "Did you see what he was using? That was a Siemens encrypted satellite radio. They're secure as hell and brand new. They run about a thousand euros apiece. NATO doesn't even use them yet."

"Well, it might have been the defense minister. Worden is the senior officer on this."

"Al," Rabble said with a pitying look, "you're the man in charge here. If the DM had called, it would have been for you."

Before Braden could respond, Worden returned and went to the cockpit. Then he finally emerged and sat beside Morley.

Braden and Rabble sat in the second row and belted in. A moment later, they heard the sound of the twin Rolls-Royce Tay 611s whining to life. Unlike an airliner, the G-IV was well insulated and the sound muted. Ann reached back and squeezed his hand. "You have a lot of clout, I see. Perhaps I should be nicer to you."

Braden squeezed back. "I'll remind you at the appropriate time."

Ann laughed. "I'm sure you will, love."

The jet turned smoothly away from the hangar. A few minutes later, they were in position at the runway threshold. After obtaining clearance from the tower, the pilots increased power. Braden felt the sudden acceleration push him into the deeply cushioned seat as the sleek jet rotated off the runway and climbed steeply into the morning sky.

"Wow, what a ride," Ann said, still gripping his hand. The jet banked to the southeast toward the Rhine River.

They heard Dacres's Gallic voice over the cabin speakers a few minutes later. "We have reached our cruising altitude of six thousand meters. You may unbuckle your belts and are free to move about the cabin. Our flight time to Wetzlar is an hour and twenty minutes."

The time passed swiftly. As the cities and factories, railyards and wharves, of the Northern Rhine gave way to vast green forests and flat farmland, the team sat at the table to discuss what they knew and what to do about it. Ann was the only person not officially part of the search for the Romans, yet she had been the catalyst for the entire investigation.

She had called him in the middle of the night more than a week before to tell him about the Roman cellar that had been discovered near Reims. Although Braden's hobby was military history, he developed a professional interest in the find when he realized that the two murdered Belgian state police officers had been killed with Roman legionary weapons. Traveling to the site, he met Morley and Sharon, who conducted him on a tour of the most extensive archaeological site since King Tut's tomb. It held the remains of more than three thousand Roman legionaries, their armor, and their weapons. But several strange anomalies added to the mystery. The entrance was a solid block of stone that could only be opened from the inside, there were several hundred bodies that appeared to have died only weeks before, and most perplexing of all was the designation of a legion that was completely unknown to historians. It was Braden who made the critical link between the seventeenth, eighteenth, and nineteenth legions that had been massacred in the Teutoburg Forest and this enigmatic fifty-fourth legion. Legio LIV's honorific, emblazoned on their shields, was Vindicta, a word that translated to revenge, vengeance, and punishment.

Then Sharon discovered that the burned plant material found in three thousand bronze bowls in the sixty sleeping chambers was an extremely powerful sleep sedative. Anyone sealed in a room with the smoke would hibernate in a deep, extended coma. These facts, tied with the bizarre events and murders, led Braden to the unavoidable conclusion that a thousand legionaries had somehow survived for two thousand years.

Then Braden, Morley, and Sharon interviewed the only survivor of the hijacked Rhine towboat, Captain Heinrich Stauffen. From Stauffen, they learned many important details of how many Romans there were, their general health and appearance, but most importantly, the name of the legion commander.

"Legatus Lucius Cassius Aquilius," Morley said as he looked over his notes. "He must be a capable and motivated officer to have gotten his men so far."

"I agree," Sharon said. "I still marvel that the legionaries haven't rebelled by now. They must know the cause they signed up for has long since vanished. They have to know that Arminius and the Germanic tribes are long dead."

Braden nodded. "I suppose the ones still alive are the most fanatical and motivated."

He was still trying to figure out where the legion was at that moment. Five nights previously, they set a large brush fire along the Autobahn near Bad Marienberg. The fire allowed them to cross the wide road and disappear into the Westerwald, a dense forest of more than 150,000 square kilometers.

Sharon was looking at her iPad. "This is interesting. One of our teams found six Roman bodies this morning. They were buried near the west bank of the Meuse River." She bit her lip, looking over the report. "Those men had to have died only a few days after leaving the cellar. The bodies we autopsied had only faint traces of Liliacae Mallorcus residue in their tissues. The bodies in the cellar had extremely high levels of it. I'm willing to bet they're dying out at a rate of ten to twenty per day now."

"How many do you think are left alive now?" General Worden asked her.

She looked out the window at the clear azure sky for a moment before replying. "Captain Stauffen said there were eight hundred Romans on the barge. If we assume about twenty men die each night, there would only be about five hundred and sixty or so left, probably less."

"Too bad we can't just wait them out," Rabble said. "Given enough time, they would all die out." He looked at the others and showed them a rueful smile. "Sorry, gang. I know you really want to find them alive. But you know our primary goal is to keep them from killing anyone else."

"I agree," Braden said. "But I really hope we find them before they all die." He glanced at the old archaeologist. "Professor Morley isn't the only one who wants to meet a real, live Roman legionary from the first century."

Then Ann spoke up. "Excuse me, but do you think that's a good idea?" Her blue eyes were wide with worry. "I mean, these men are dangerous. You told me the Roman legions were the best fighting force in history. They'll kill anyone who even gets close to them."

Braden squeezed her hand. "Yes, they were, but these men are a special case. I think Lucius has acted pretty civilized so far. He's had plenty of opportunities to kill innocent people. He let that man who saw them on the river go, and that girl who saw them by the brush fire was allowed to live too."

"But they did kill some people," Ann protested.

Morley nodded. "Yes, Miss Hamilton, but that may have been unavoidable. We know that one of the Belgian policemen threatened them and fired his pistol. Five legionaries were killed by gunfire. The Romans probably killed in self-defense. And as for the towboat crew, one of them shot at Lucius before he was killed. I don't know how the others died, but anything can happen in such a chaotic situation." He rubbed his chin. "I agree with Alex. I don't think the Romans will kill without cause. They're on a specific mission."

It was Braden's turn to nod. "If we can find them and talk with Lucius, he might see reason and lay down his arms." He looked at Morley. "Professor, your Latin skills would be the key to that."

"I hope you're right, Alex," Morley said. He rubbed his eyes. "But we have to find them first."

At that moment, the computer on the bulkhead table chimed. "Sounds like we have a message from headquarters," Braden said as he turned his chair to face the monitor. After accessing the secure network, he took a moment to read. "Well, I'll be damned." The others around the table looked at him. "One of the search helicopters was hit by an arrow."

For a long moment no one spoke. Then Rabble said, "When?"

Braden scanned the rest of the message. "The night they stumbled on the nudist camp. Someone discovered it this morning during a maintenance stand-down. The arrowhead was embedded in the helicopter's belly."

Sharon's eyes were wide. "Are they sure?"

Braden opened an image of a bent iron arrowhead and a few centimeters of the broken shaft. "It looks like the ones they found near the fires."

Morley leaned over to see. "Bloody hell," he muttered. "It's Roman."

"The chopper must have flown right over Lucius and his legion," Braden said.

"Very close, Alex," Morley responded, unable to tear his eyes from the picture.

"Could an arrow stick in a metal helicopter hull?" Worden asked.

Braden answered for Morley. "Oh, believe me, it can. Roman bows were strong, like Welsh longbows. A draw weight of almost a hundred pounds. Loosed straight up, it could easily pierce the thin aluminum skin of a low-flying helicopter."

Rabble rubbed his lower lip. "The only time that arrow could have hit the chopper was when they descended to about fifty meters just before jumping the nudist camp." He walked over to his briefcase to retrieve a topographical map of the Westerwald. Unfolding it on the table, he pointed to a spot west of the mountains. "Right about here is where the nudist camp was." He examined the map more closely. "Just to the west is this small ravine. It's perfect for the Romans to hide in."

Braden felt a wave of frustration. "They were right there. Damn it! If only we'd known about their lower body temperature." He saw Sharon looking at him and immediately felt guilty. "I'm sorry, Sharon. It's not your fault. We were all too confident."

She gave him a half-smile. "Don't sweat it, Alex. Live and learn."

Morley looked over the map. "They could be in the mountains by now. They probably moved out quickly after the helicopter left."

Braden nodded. "I bet they did. Now they're going to be a lot harder to find."

The whine of the twin engines changed. "We're going to begin our descent into Wetzlar," Captain Dacres announced. "Please fasten your seatbelts." The Gulfstream banked steeply to the left. Braden looked down from his lofty perch and saw the vast green carpet of the Westerwald passing below. Looking ahead of the wing, he saw serried ranks of ridges and bare rock protruding from the forests, ending at the peaks of the Rothaar Mountains. Beyond that were open meadows and wooded areas.

"See any Romans?" Rabble asked.

"They're down there," Braden said soberly. "I know it."

The Westphalian city of Wetzlar lay on a forested plain just beyond the foothills. The Gulfstream lined up on final approach, and with surprising gentleness, the wheels touched down on the runway as the thrust reversers howled to slow the jet. A minute after landing, the engines went silent. Captain Dacres walked to the rear door and opened it. A rush of warm air filled the cabin. Braden stood, glancing at Rabble. "Here we go, Barn."

"After you, pal," Rabble said, stepping aside with a slight bow.

They emerged into the midmorning sunlight of a clear, warm summer day. The air was tinged with the scent of evergreen and the tang of jet exhaust.

"Looks like the fuzz is here," Rabble said, pointing at two tan vans waiting a few meters away. "Schroeder is with them."

Braden put on a pair of sunglasses and helped Ann down the steps. "Welcome to Germany, honey."

She put on her sunglasses. "How lovely it is here. Look at those mountains. You don't see that color green in England."

Rabble grinned. "Well, I said we're going to Oz. And there is the Emerald City."

Braden looked to the west. The mountains were an imposing gray rampart nestled in a green mantle of evergreen forests. Somewhere up there was Lucius Cassius Aquilius, the legatus of the last Roman Legion on earth. A legion whose sole reason for existence was to kill as many Germans as possible.

Braden felt a chill even in the warm summer air. *And I've put myself and my friends right in his sights. Now, he'll be hunting us.*

CHAPTER I

CORRELATION OF FORCE

Landespolizei Commissioner Karl Schroeder shook Rabble's hand. He was a large man with a pronounced waistline only partially concealed by a neatly tailored dark gray jacket and slacks. A pair of gold-rimmed sunglasses hid his deep-set eyes. "Herr Rabble, good to see you again."

"And you too, Herr Commissioner," Rabble said.

Braden, standing behind Rabble, was amused that his friend was so chummy with the Landespolizei commissioner. Only a week before, Karl Schroeder had been acerbic, combative, and downright hostile during the first briefing at NATO Headquarters. His jurisdiction was the entire North Rhine and Westphalia region.

Then, a short, petite woman of about forty with black hair stepped forward. She wore the neat gray-green uniform of the Landespolizei. Schroeder made the introductions. "May I introduce Colonel Hanna Ortmann. She is the local Landespolizei commander."

Ortmann smiled, holding out her hand to Rabble. "I'm glad to meet you, Herr Rabble. I trust your flight was pleasant?" Her accent was pure Bavarian, with clear consonants and long vowels.

"Yes, Colonel," Rabble said, stepping aside for Braden. "This is Alex Braden, the driving force behind our . . . project."

"Thank you for meeting us, Colonel," Braden said, shaking her hand. She had a surprisingly strong grip for a woman who could not have weighed more than sixty kilograms. "I'm grateful for your help."

"Well, that remains to be seen," she said, glancing at Schroeder. "Commissioner Schroeder requested that I provide more security for this event, but I'm still not sure what you expect of me."

"I realize this is an unorthodox situation, but we believe there's a real danger to the rally. And we want to help assure the safety of the officials and the public."

"We shall see what can be done." Ortmann waved for the vans to come over. "We'll discuss the security arrangements on the way. I think you'll see there's little more to do." She climbed in beside the uniformed driver as the luggage was loaded into the rear.

"I hope to see just that," Braden said, taking a seat behind her. Rabble sat beside him while Schroeder and Worden took the rear bench seat. Sharon, Morley, and Ann entered the second van. They drove off the airport tarmac, through a gate, and headed north through the small city of Wetzlar. The town had old-world German character with steep rooflines and ornate church steeples, inns, and hotels liberally dotting the low-wooded foothills. The streets were virtually empty, and Braden realized most residents and local businesses were at the rally. A few kilometers further, the driver turned onto a new road, the A60, which bore a sign proclaiming *Nationaler Natur-Park von Westphalen, 22 Km.*

"We will be there in about twenty minutes," said Ortmann. "The Westerwald's eastern frontier is to our left. The low mountain range you see is the southern end of the Rothaar Mountains."

Braden regarded the distant green barrier denoting the edge of the vast forest. The trees were as thick as the fur on a dog, and hills rose in long slopes until they crested in a steep ridge that faded into the morning haze to the north.

In a short time, they passed large parking areas solidly packed with cars and campers. People of all ages were dressed in shorts, jeans, bright shirts, and caps. Some carried coolers or pushed strollers filled with children toward the huge park's natural arena. The van drove under a tall sign formed by towering logs with the park's name in bright yellow letters on a dark green sign.

During the flight, Braden had studied a brochure on the park. It opened in 2019 amid great fanfare. Everything from rock concerts to Boy Scout jamborees used the year-round facilities and beautiful natural surroundings. As far as he could see were dozens of colorful tents and booths selling everything from flags to hats to Coca-Cola and beer.

"The public has been arriving since the day before yesterday," Ortmann said. "They expect more than forty thousand people to attend. The parking areas are filling rapidly, the campsites are fully occupied, and the concessions are doing a good business."

Braden nodded. "When will the chancellor's party arrive?"

"In about two hours." A Landespolizei officer walking among the concessions saw the van passing and waved to Ortmann. She returned it. "We put our teams out yesterday."

Braden saw people carrying the flags of Germany, the United States, the United Nations, and NATO. He also noted some groups waving placards with "NATO Raus! Deutschland für Deutsches!" and a large one with "Keine Fremderen Soldaten auf Deutschem Boden."

"'No more foreign soldiers on German soil,'" Rabble muttered. "Idiots."

A television news team was interviewing the protestors. The van passed several international news service vans and RVs with satellite dishes sprouting from their roofs like silver flowers.

"There are a large number of Germans who feel strongly about the presence of NATO in our country," Schroeder said. "I cannot say I disagree with them."

Worden grunted. "Such narrow-minded sentiments will lead only to disaster."

Schroeder glared at him. "Disaster, General? How can you say that having armed foreign military forces in Germany is still justified now that the Warsaw Pact is kaput?"

"There are still many enemies of democracy and freedom in the world, Herr Commissioner."

For the next few kilometers, the two men remained quiet, but it was obvious to Braden that Schroeder was still vehemently anti-NATO. He was glad Worden was there to keep the police officer from resuming his harangue.

They arrived at a restricted parking area near the park's western edge. In the distance, a huge natural amphitheater surrounded a large stage and grassy plain where tall speaker silos sprouted like medieval siege towers. Thousands of people sat on the benches or on blankets and folding chairs, drinking, eating, and watching children play in the summer sun. It looked more like a rock music festival than a political rally. Behind the stage was a tall wooden tower, at least fifty meters high, studded with giant high-definition Jumbotrons and lights.

"Here we are," Ortmann said, getting out of the van. She led Braden and the others to a trailer like the ones used at construction sites. "This is our mobile command post. We can coordinate our phase of security from here."

"Good," Worden said, heading for the trailer's door. "Let's see what you have to show us." Braden noticed that the German officer was more taciturn than usual, as if he were irritated at dealing with something out of his responsibility. He chalked it up to the animosity between Worden and Schroeder.

The others followed Worden inside, and Braden turned to Ann. "Honey, this might take a while. Do you want to come in or get something to eat?"

She looked at the many rows of souvenir and food concessions a hundred meters away. "Oh, I think I'll find something to keep me occupied." After a kiss on Braden's cheek, she scampered off.

The trailer was a command post on wheels, with printers, faxes, computers, maps, phones, and coffee machines. A series of monitors displayed scenes of the park, the roads, the amphitheater and stage, entrances, and other locations. A dozen officers worked at the computers, taking radio calls.

Ortmann looked at Braden. "I have been informed there are live Romans out there, probably in the Westerwald, and they present a threat to the public. Is that right?"

"Yes," Braden said. "We're concerned for the safety of the thousands of people here."

Ortmann led him to a large map on one wall. "Let's lay everything out in the open. Commissioner Schroeder convinced the federal and local police officials to allow us to patrol the park's outer boundaries. More than two hundred mobile armed officers are patrolling the park and public areas. We can coordinate with them but cannot interfere with their security arrangements."

"Yes," said Schroeder, pouring a cup of coffee from a carafe. "They do not have any objections to our patrols of the boundaries but are adamant that we stay out of their way."

Braden almost smiled. "As long as your people can protect the land around the park and between it and the Westerwald, I'm satisfied. Thank you, Herr Commissioner."

Schroeder nodded. "It wasn't easy, but we have almost a hundred men and women out there."

Worden spoke up. "I see your security cameras cover nearly the entire rally area."

"Yes," Ortmann said. "The park has an extensive network of cameras. We were allowed to link our monitors to them. As Commissioner Schroeder said, we have almost one hundred officers in trucks patrolling the park borders in constant radio contact."

"What is their patrol pattern?" Worden asked, peering at the map.

Ortmann examined a sheaf of papers. "Half of the force is set up in five teams of ten troopers. They are concentrated on the western perimeter of the park. All along here," she said, pointing at the line that delineated the park boundaries.

Braden mulled this over. "So there are about three hundred officers from three separate law enforcement branches handling the security?" He thought Lucius's legion far outnumbered them.

Ortmann nodded. "Correct. There will be five hundred troops at the rally, but none will be armed. That's standard procedure in this type of situation, I believe."

"Correct," Worden said simply. "It is too dangerous to have loaded automatic weapons around all those civilians."

"Are your officers able to deal with any threat?" Braden asked.

Ortmann gave him a long look. "They carry riot gear and weapons. If they see a potential threat, they call in a Code Red with the coordinates. A dispatcher," she pointed to a pair of uniformed women at a console with computers and phones, "will alert the response team. Two of the ten-man units will immediately converge in trucks to the site of the threat and set up a defensive barrier."

Worden frowned. "How fast can they react?"

"The reaction force can be onsite in less than ten minutes," Ortmann said confidently.

Braden bit his lip. "Colonel Ortmann, please forgive me, but a lot of people can die in ten minutes."

The Landespolizei colonel did not seem offended. It spoke volumes about her professionalism. "What do you suggest?"

"Could the reaction team be stationed at the west gate until the rally is over?"

Ortmann looked at Schroeder before responding. "I suppose we can do that." Leaning over the shoulder of one of the dispatchers, she said, "Call Captain Bach. Tell him his orders have changed. The reaction teams are to take over the west gate post."

Then she turned back to Braden and the others. "Is that sufficient?"

Braden felt relieved. "Yes, thank you."

Worden rubbed his lower lip as if deep in thought. "They should not interfere with any other units inside the park itself."

Ortmann turned to him. "They have their area of responsibility; we have ours."

Rabble looked at the banks of monitors. "I understand the concern about the German and American Army battalions being unarmed, but it would be a sad state of affairs if the Romans attacked the rally and all the soldiers could do was swear at them."

Braden was glad Rabble had brought it up.

Ortmann shook her head. "That is out of my hands, I'm afraid. The orders come directly from the Defense Ministry."

"Still," Rabble persisted, looking at her. "I wish there were some way to have ammo available just in case. The American M-16 and German

G36 rifles use the same 5.56-millimeter cartridge. The Gebirgsjäger alone would be more than a match for a Roman Legion. They're elite troops."

"Yes," Schroeder said. "The best alpine troops in the world."

Braden noted a tone of pride in the police official's voice.

"How many Romans do you think are out there?" Ortmann asked.

Sharon, who had been watching the exchange, spoke up. "At least five hundred. There may be more."

Worden looked at Rabble. "There will be no ammunition for the Gebirgsjäger or American battalions. That is final."

Braden saw Rabble regarding Worden with a speculative look. He pursed his lips in what might have been the first letter of "Bullshit." But he remained silent.

Worden continued, "The soldiers are coming to be part of the chancellor's honor guard, not to fight Romans."

"Where are they right now?" Rabble asked.

"The Gebirgsjäger are on the B45," Worden said, checking his watch. "Right now, they're about to stop in Limburg for a rest. Their ETA is in three hours. The Americans are on the A60. They'll arrive in a few minutes."

Braden looked up at the wall map. He saw the double blue line that denoted the A60 entering the park from the west. He felt a cold chill as the mental image of a column of unarmed soldiers traveling through the dense and vast Westerwald, unknowingly entering the lair of a legion of desperate armed Romans bent on attacking a military target. "They're coming in on the A60 through the Westerwald?"

The general nodded. "That is correct."

Morley, silent up to this point, suddenly looked alarmed. "The Romans! Suppose they attack the army troops?"

Ortmann and Schroeder exchanged worried looks at this. "Is that possible?" the commissioner asked. "Can they hurt the Gebirgsjäger battalion?"

Braden was about to reply, but Morley spoke first. "A column of military trucks would be a tempting target for the Romans."

"How would men who lived two thousand years ago recognize a modern army unit?" Worden asked.

Braden said, "A long column of identical trucks carrying men all dressed the same is pretty obvious. An army looks like an army."

"We have no proof that they are near the road," Worden said. "In any event, how could a band of men armed with swords harm a convoy of heavy trucks traveling on a road?"

It was Sharon's turn to speak. "They're very good at combat and ambush, General. Don't underestimate them. Also, they were ambushed on a road in the Teutoburg Forest. I'm sure they'd love to return the favor."

Braden hadn't thought of that, but he suddenly realized Sharon was right. He reached up and ran a finger along the blue line that denoted the A60 winding its way up the mountains. "They could be waiting for the moment to attack."

Rabble looked back and forth between the three Germans. "Look, this is getting us nowhere. Can you call and warn the Gebirgsjäger battalion that they should be alert for an ambush?"

The question hung in the warm air of the trailer for several seconds. Only the sound of computer keyboards and the occasional squelch of a radio call broke the silence.

Ortmann was first to speak. "I have no authority over the army units. They are fully under the Defense Ministry."

Schroeder, who had been looking at the map with an expression of deep concern on his face, shook his head. "Colonel Ortmann is correct. I could only get the Defense Ministry to agree to the Landespolizei's participation if we did not involve ourselves with military operations." He gritted his teeth. "Insanity."

Rabble looked at Worden, who stood with his arms folded. "General, can you contact the Gebirgsjäger and warn them to be on the alert?"

Worden rubbed his chin again. "I do not dare make a call about the Romans on an open radio frequency. If the media intercepted the call, all hell would break loose."

"God, what a disaster that would be," Morley said.

Rabble persisted. "Don't you have a secure link to the Gebirgsjäger's command frequency? The media won't overhear that."

Worden shook his head. "Unfortunately, no. I do not have a direct connection with the army units. Only the rally organizers at park head-quarters have direct communications with them." He sighed. "An over-sight on my part, I'm afraid. I'm sorry."

Schroeder shot him a hard look. "So call the park organizers and ask them to relay a warning to the column. You don't even have to mention the Romans. Only tell them to be alert. Say anti-NATO factions may try to intercept them or interfere with the rally." He shook his head at the irony. "Well, that would be right."

Worden finally nodded. "Very well," he said. "I will call the park headquarters and ask that the warning be passed on." He glanced at his watch. "The American battalion is probably nearly here. I will see that the Gebirgsjäger is alerted."

"Also, ask them to report if they see anything odd," Braden suggested.

"Odd?" Ortmann asked as she looked out the wide window. Outside were tens of thousands of people in multicolored clothes, waving flags, banners, and balloons. Bare-chested men and women danced to rock music from their portable stereos. She had a wry smile on her face. "I think they can count on it, Herr Braden."

The drive north had lasted most of the night, and Private Helmut Schroeder's butt felt as if he'd been sitting on a concrete block. He grimaced, trying to get more comfortable. At least they'd gotten some sleep. Major Bentele chartered the use of three barracks rooms at a large youth hostelry outside Frankfurt from 2100 to 0400. After using the institutional bathrooms, the tired and sore soldiers laid their sleeping bags on the double bunks and instantly fell asleep. After a hasty washing and shaving, they wolfed down boxed breakfasts and resumed the journey. That had been three hours earlier.

Helmut was in his second year with Gebirgsjäger Battalion 232. It was absolutely the best posting in the entire Bundeswehr. As one of the truly elite mountain troops, he took pride in his appearance and duty. He worshipped the battalion commander, Lieutenant Colonel Eugen Koll, a man who took good care of his troops. He often entered the barracks to chat with the privates and non-commissioned officers. It was rare for a German Army field-grade officer to be so familiar with his troops, but Koll did things his own way. It paid off. The unit had earned five awards for efficiency and morale. Helmut bent to check that his G36 rifle was safely stowed under the bench next to his rucksack, then pulled his phone out of the side of his shoulder bag. He was surprised to find a text message from his Uncle Karl. He read it over and smiled. His uncle was already at the rally. It would be the first time Karl Schroeder would see his only nephew with Gebirgsjäger Battalion 232. He quickly tapped in a response.

Uncle Karl, that is great news. Come and find us when we get there.

Putting the phone away, he looked around the interior of the army truck.

Corporal Ernst Walther was reading *Stern* magazine. Helmut caught a glimpse of a half-nude woman as the corporal turned a page.

"Limburg in five minutes," said the co-driver, leaning in from the window to the cab. "Walther and Kranz, get your men assembled as soon as we park."

"Ja, Sergeant," the corporals said in unison. Walther folded the magazine and slipped it into his bag.

"About time," one private grunted. "I need a latrine."

"And a bath," said another voice. "I've been smelling your armpits since yesterday."

"At least I use deodorant, Krueger," said the first man.

"Could have fooled me," Walther said, sotto voce. "I suppose I'll have to restore some order here. Let's get ready so we can have the most time out of the truck. Schroeder, you find the latrines."

"Toilets, they're called in the civilian world," said Corporal Kranz.

Helmut smiled. That was fine with him. "Jawohl, Corporal. My pleasure."

A few minutes later, they heard the deep thrum of the diesel engine change pitch. The truck slowed and turned to the right. Then it stopped and the engine went silent. "All out," yelled the driver. "One hour for rations and latrine. Change into the new fatigues and boots."

The two men closest to the rear unlatched the tailgate. Outside it was a bright sunny morning with blue skies and fragrant breezes. The next truck pulled in as Helmut jumped to the ground, carrying his bag. He stretched his legs. It felt wonderful to move again. Behind him, he heard Walther's sharp voice calling, "Fall in! Rausch! Krueger, you guard the truck. I'll relieve you in ten minutes."

A detail of troops put a rope barrier around the battalion's trucks. The rest area was huge, with plenty of space. A dozen or so civilian cars and campers dotted the parking area, and children ran over to see the soldiers.

The rest area contained a cafeteria, laundromat, and showers. Helmut found the neat, green-painted building with the international symbols for Dammen and Herren. He took advantage of being first and, in a minute, had emerged to rejoin his comrades. "The latrines are just past that picnic area," he told Walther. "Ten commodes, six urinals, and six sinks."

The corporal nodded. "Fall out and hit the latrines," he said to his men. "Back here in twenty." With more than three hundred men wanting to use the latrines, it could have been chaos, but German Army discipline reigned, and soon the men were lined up by the chow truck to receive their boxed lunches. They could choose either a thick meat sandwich and fruit or cold meat stew and bread.

Helmut sat in the picnic area next to Walther. Every table was packed with soldiers while others sat on the clean grass. "It feels good to get out of that truck for a while," he said, taking a bite of a ham sandwich.

"Enjoy it while you can," Walther said, popping a slice of apple into his mouth.

"I heard some people might make trouble at the rally. There have been some nasty demonstrations around the country."

"That's why they want us there," Helmut said. "We're the elite truppen of the army."

Kranz shook his head. "But we're not even armed."

"Orders," Walther said, finishing his fruit.

Helmut nodded. "I just hope we don't run into anything we can't handle. An empty G36 rifle isn't much of a deterrent."

Checking his watch, Walther said, "I think I'll get changed now."

"Right behind you, Corporal." Helmut gathered their trash and tossed it one-handed into a nearby can. He regarded the soldiers who had taken advantage of the warm sun to catch some sleep. "I'll help Corporal Kranz get the 'elite truppen' up from their nappy."

As the young soldier walked to the restroom to change his uniform, he noticed a man in a blue Mercedes parked outside the barrier tape. He was talking on a large cell phone. As Helmut passed the open side window of the car, he heard the man's voice. "—they will be moving in a few minutes. I will. Observer Three out." Then the man saw the Gebirgsjäger soldier walking by and tossed him a casual salute. "*Guten Morgen*, Private."

Helmut smiled and returned the gesture. But as he reached the restroom door, he couldn't help thinking the man looked as though he'd been caught in an illegal act. He glanced back, but the Mercedes was no longer there.

In twenty minutes, the convoy again headed northwest.

Horst Molders listened to the radio call less than sixty kilometers to the south. "Understood, Observer Three. Keep your distance. Panzer Two out." He turned in the seat. "Observer Three reports the Gebirgsjäger battalion has just left the Limburg rest stop. They are fifty-two minutes ahead of schedule."

Hauser checked the map. "Very well. We'll have to speed up. The A60 is thirty kilometers from the Limburg stop. Call the truck drivers and tell them to accelerate to ninety kilometers per hour." He picked up his radio. "Panzer One to Panzer Three. We are accelerating to nine-zero kph. Acknowledge. Over."

"Copy," Mathias Kiel said from the trailing staff car. "Nine-zero kph."

From behind the wheel, Hans Becker pressed the BMW's accelerator pedal and set the cruise control to ninety kilometers per hour. He checked his rear-view mirror to make sure the trucks kept their proper interval.

Hauser tapped on his calculator. "If we maintain this speed for one hour, we'll have gained forty-five minutes. The Gebirgsjäger will be no more than twelve to fifteen minutes ahead of us." He continued looking at the map. "How much distance is Observer Three maintaining?"

Molders responded without turning. "One or two kilometers, depending on the terrain. He can see the truck column, but they can't see him among the normal traffic." Molders looked back at Hauser. "He'll have to break off in a few more minutes. The mountains will make it hard for him to keep the army trucks in sight unless he closes in. That's too risky. An officer might see him and become suspicious."

Hauser nodded. "By then it shouldn't matter." The NOD leader let his gaze wander to the world outside. The rolling green countryside of west-central Germany was bathed in the cool light of midmorning. Prevailing winds from the west had blown a cool mist from the Rhine Valley. Persistent patches of hazy drizzle evaporated as the sun rose over the forests to the east. *We're almost there,* Hauser thought. He felt a quickening in his chest as their moment drew ever closer. *The destiny of New Germania awaits.*

He turned to look behind the staff car. The three hundred and thirty armed men in those seventeen trucks were the striking arm of the New Order of Deutschland. For more than twenty years, Hauser and the nucleus of the NOD had been working toward removing all foreign business and military encroachment in Germany. Hauser had a personal interest in freeing Germany from the NATO alliance. His father had been killed when an out-of-control American Abrams tank ran over him—a defining moment in young Josef's life.

From that day on, he had been a man possessed. By finding and recruiting other Germans who felt likewise, Hauser assembled what was now the most powerful terrorist army in the world. More than five hundred former army soldiers and law enforcement officers had been rigorously trained and equipped in a secret facility in the Hunsrück Mountains. Clad in authentic uniforms and carrying the standard-issue Heckler & Koch G36 automatic rifles, they were now about to play their role as the doppelganger of Gebirgsjäger Battalion 232.

Every detail of the operation had been worked out, even to painting the correct unit numbers on the trucks. No one, not even a Bundeswehr veteran, could tell that the NOD troop convoy was anything but the real thing. The only difference was that Hauser's men were fully armed with bandoliers of live ammunition. And they had every intention of using it when they attacked and overwhelmed the security troops protecting Hoffman and the officials at the rally.

The NOD's three hundred armed troops would hold Chancellor Hoffman and key members of his cabinet hostage. Even better, they would have thousands of men, women, and children as human shields. From this unassailable bargaining position, Hauser and the NOD would finally force the government and people of Germany to return to the hereditary path they had left a century ago.

He glanced at his watch again. "No plan ever survives first contact with the enemy," he muttered. In this case, the enemy was time. They had to follow the Gebirgsjäger up the A60 to the park's west entrance, and timing was crucial. The NOD trucks must roll into the park no more than ten minutes after the real battalion. Hauser had a full set of forged papers to show the park gate personnel. Just another of the dozens of military units that were part of the rally.

Mathias Kiel, a former Bundeswehr sergeant who had trained the NOD soldiers, would lead the first fifty armed troops to surround the chancellor's party before the Gebirgsjäger or Americans were assembled for their parade. Another one hundred men under Horst Molders would disarm the police and security teams while a like number spread out to take control of the media and communications units. A special squad of troops, led by Anton Mannheim, was tasked with surrounding the central amphitheater and maintaining control of the civilians. There was no way to know how many hostages would be in the amphitheater, but Houser's estimates put the number above fifteen thousand. It would indeed be the dawn of a new Germany.

If we get there in time. Hauser looked at his watch again, trying not to show his increasing apprehension.

CHAPTER II

WAITING GAMES

The road ahead of the Gebirgsjäger truck column wound its way into the hills, and tall evergreen groves gave way to the dense forests of the Westerwald.

In the lead BMW staff car, Lieutenant Colonel Eugen Koll checked the time and his iPad. He was confident they'd arrive at the rally at least an hour early. "We're making good time," he said to his aide, Captain Weber, who was reading over the rally schedule.

Weber nodded. "We will arrive with time to spare. The men can use it to clean up."

The staff car crested a ridge and followed the winding two-lane highway through the forest. The trees were thick on both sides, punctuated with small farms and open fields. It was pretty country. Koll said, "What do you make of that call from General Worden?"

Weber shrugged. "We knew the anti-NATO factions were going to be at the rally. I suppose they might try to disrupt things."

"That could backfire on them," Koll observed. "The world media will be watching." He rubbed the back of his neck. The sun was streaming through the rear window. "Nevertheless, we'll be alert. The Americans will have been told too."

"They are in greater danger than we," said Weber. "Even the anti-NATO fanatics love us."

Koll laughed. "Love from fools like that I can do without."

"Everything will go just fine," Weber said, looking out the windows.

Just then, a beeping tone came from the car's radio. Weber punched the speaker button. "Weber here."

"This is Sergeant Klausmeyer in Truck 11. We're having some engine trouble. Over."

Koll shook his head. The captain tried not to meet his superior's eyes. "What kind of trouble? Do you require emergency assistance? Over."

"The radiator temperature is almost to the red line. I think it's the thermostat. It'll just require some time to cool. Over."

Weber asked, "How much time do you think we'll need, Klausmeyer?"

"It's not yet critical. But we're approaching the mountains. I'd feel better if we could take about half an hour to cool down before we start climbing."

Weber looked at Koll, who nodded. "We can afford the time. Let's look for another turnout, and we'll stop for half an hour. Pass the word to the column."

"Klausmeyer," Weber said, "we will stop at the next turnout." He switched to the battalion frequency. "All trucks, we will be making an unscheduled stop at the next turnout. Be ready to deploy in standard mode. Weber out."

Koll peered through the windshield and said to the driver, "Do you see anything up ahead?"

Sergeant Dorfman waited before replying. "I think there's a large one on the B45 in about a kilometer. I saw it from the last rise. It's about ten kilometers before the junction with the A60." He glanced at the GPS, whose screen was blank. He tapped it and the unit came back on. *Shit. Bad batteries. Just what I need.*

"That will be fine," Koll said.

"I'll call Sergeant Haaber," said Weber. "He's the best mechanic in the battalion."

Koll smirked. "Weber, you have been a soldier long enough to know that saying 'everything will be fine' is a curse."

"Yes, Colonel," the aide said with a grin. "Never again."

A few minutes later, Dorfman slowed the car and slid neatly off the blacktop into a large gravel-surfaced turnout. It was the size of a large sports field, just enough for the battalion's trucks. He drove to the far end, making sure he was well clear of the area the vehicles would need for parking.

Watching over his shoulder, Koll saw the first of the trucks stop a few meters behind them, angled toward the road. The second truck did the same, coming to a stop behind the first. In less than five minutes, the column was off the road and in place.

"Okay, we can take some time to check our gear," Koll said to Weber. "You go and check Klausmeyer's truck."

"Yes, Colonel," the captain said, exiting the BMW.

Koll walked around the car, inhaling the clean mountain air, only slightly tinged with the smell of diesel exhaust. He saw a long north-south ridge rising in the distance. He watched Weber stop at one of the trucks in line. Another man stepped down from the cab and followed the officer to the eleventh truck.

Major Bentele walked up. "Colonel, do you want to inform the gate at the rally we will be delayed?"

Koll thought a moment. "No, Major, it's not necessary. We'll be on time. I don't want to give them any reason for concern."

Private Helmut Schroeder climbed out of the second truck, glad for the change in routine. "Ah, that feels good. What's the delay?"

Corporal Walther grunted. "The driver said one of the trucks has some engine trouble. We'll stop for about half an hour."

"I don't have a problem with that," his junior comrade said with a smile.

At that point a sergeant came over and conferred with Walther. A moment later he jogged off to the next truck in line.

"What was that all about?" Helmut said, looking at the frown on the corporal's face.

"He said that Colonel Koll told all the drivers and co-drivers to be alert when we enter the forest."

"What for?" Helmut automatically turned to look into the woods on the other side of the road.

"He didn't say specifically," Walther said, also scanning the forest. "Just some concerns about anti-NATO lunatics who might ambush us."

Helmut laughed, but then he looked at the canvas sides of the truck. "That wouldn't be difficult. We're blind in the back. And that canvas is about as bulletproof as latrine paper."

Braden and Ann walked through the attractions and concessions. The weather was warm with a gentle breeze from the west. The sky hung over them like a great azure bell. Birds flitted through the evergreens and fought over peanuts and popcorn on the ground. Thousands of people walked or rode bicycles along the neat paths bordering small lakes and picnic areas. Everywhere was the sound of laughter, music, and speeches.

They passed displays of German, French, British, and American tanks and infantry fighting vehicles. Children received tours of the armored vehicles and were allowed to sit in the drivers' seats. There were soldiers in battle dress uniforms talking to the public and demonstrations of high-technology equipment and weapons. Large video screens showed battle maneuvers and the history of NATO. Booths handed out free stickers, toy planes, and tanks to the kids and pamphlets and recruitment applications to the adults.

Braden bought them each a large sports cup with ice and soda. The long row of food concessions sold drinks, sandwiches, pastries, sausages, and ice cream to the crowd. The air was ripe with a myriad of smells and aromas. Long lines of patrons jammed the walkways around the central amphitheater.

"I can't believe how big this event is," Ann said beside him. "The telly has been blabbering on about it for the last week, but I didn't realize so many people were interested in supporting NATO."

Braden looked at her with a smirk. "I'm glad some people do." He took a long drink of cold soda. "But don't be fooled. Most of these folks really don't care about NATO one way or another. They're here for a good show. Entertainment," he said as two young bare-breasted women walked past them, "is where you find it."

She batted him playfully on the arm. "You silly clot. You never could resist a pair of boobs."

The rally was certainly a success. Chancellor Hoffman, who would be arriving in a short time, would be pleased. The gate tally was already past 35,000 people, with more arriving every hour.

A prime target. The thought leaped unbidden into his mind.

"Penny for your thoughts, love." Ann's voice cut into his reverie.

He turned to her. "Just thinking." He tried to put it out of his mind, but the plain fact remained. They still hadn't found the Romans.

"About the Romans? I thought you said they can't get here without being stopped by the police."

"Logically, I know that," he said. "But we still don't know where they are or what they plan to do. Time is running out for them." He sighed. "They have to be getting desperate. And desperate men are dangerous."

A pair of police officers with sidearms and radios passed them with smiles and polite nods. Braden had noted the strong police presence. There was no doubt the park and local police forces were watching over the rally. Schroeder and Ortmann's Landespolizei teams were patrolling the areas outside the public arenas.

Ann smiled, squeezing his hand. "The police know what they're doing. Let's just try and have a good time. This is a bit of a holiday for us, love. We can at least see this big rally." She looked at a program. "Hoffman speaks at one-thirty, followed by a ceremonial parade by the honor guard. Then there'll be a flyover of jets at three o'clock. I want to see that." Ann Hamilton's father had been in the Royal Air Force, and she liked military aircraft. "And tonight, military bands will be performing with fireworks."

Braden showed her a smile that masked his inner feelings. "I'll try, honey."

Half an hour later, satiated with food and needing to sit down, they left the main amphitheater area and went through a guarded gate. Braden asked the park guard where the Landespolizei's staging area was. The guard, dressed in a green fatigue uniform, examined Braden's NATO credentials and pointed beyond a parking area filled with concession trucks and media vans. "Just past the emergency medical infirmary, sir."

Braden thanked the man as he and Ann threaded their way through the vehicles and equipment. "Way out in the boonies," he muttered.

They found a large marquee tent over several folding tables and chairs. Morley and Sharon were at one of the tables, sipping cold drinks. "Ah," Morley said, smiling as they entered. "You found the Black Hole of Calcutta, I see." His eyes twinkled.

"Yes, we did," Braden said as they entered the cool shade. "Anything new?"

Two Landespolizei officers were filling drink cups from a row of tall coolers.

One of them, an older man with captain's insignia on his collar, shook his head. "Not so far. Our patrols report nothing unusual."

"Are you sure?" Braden asked, feeling more frustration. "There has to be something."

"Sorry," the officer said. "The radios have been silent."

Braden nodded. "Thank you . . ."

"Bach. Rudolf Bach," the officer said, extending his hand. "You are Herr Braden, I take it?"

"Yes. Sorry to be so insistent. I'm just concerned for the safety of the public."

"As am I," Bach said, smiling. "My family is here today. My wife, Hilda; my son; and two daughters. I wish for nothing to happen to them." Bach put his cap on. "Now, if you'll excuse me, I must return to my post." He offered a polite salute and left the tent.

Braden watched him go. He did not feel comforted. If anything, he was even more restless. "I can't just sit here. I have to do something."

Morley chuckled. "I feel the same way. But we have no idea where to look. And nothing has been seen or heard of them since the fires."

Sharon gave them both a level look. "I hate to say it, but we have to accept the possibility that they're already dead."

Braden shook his head in resignation. "I hope not."

Morley looked at him. "What do you think Lucius is doing right now?"

"I wish I knew, Professor." He looked to the west, wondering what the thick woods hid from his view. "I really wish I knew. Probably doing what we are. Waiting."

"We are ready, Sire," said Marcus. He and Lucius stood together as the legion finished their preparations.

"Yes, we are," his legatus replied proudly. "The legionaries have worked very hard."

Lucius Cassius Aquilius was now in his fortieth year. It had been a long, long time since the twenty-year-old Lucius first joined the Roman Army in Gallicae and worked his way up the ranks to become centurio of Princeps Prior of Cohort Tertius in Legio XVIII. That legion and two others under the command of Publius Quinctilius Varus had been ambushed and viciously slaughtered in a dark, swampy forest by the traitor Arminius and his rebellious Germanic countrymen. Only a few hundred of the more than 25,000 legionaries and civilians escaped to return to Rome. One of them was Lucius, an old veteran of thirty-six. In his heart burned a deep, hot desire for revenge.

That seed germinated and grew into the daring and dangerous plan to assemble a new legion for the express purpose of returning to Germania to destroy Arminius and his traitorous army. In the Gallicae cellar, Legio LIV Vindicta went into a deep, dreamless hibernation. But unknown to the legion, a full score of centuries passed while Rome fell and the world changed.

Of the 4,800 officers and legionaries that had begun the Somnum, only 1,100 survived. The rest were little more than bone and dust. They emerged into an incomprehensibly dangerous world of noise and lights, flying machines and strange perils. Unable to parade with their standard before them, the legion marched by night and concealed itself in the woods by day. Many died along the way to be hastily buried in pits and common graves. Among them was Septimus Deo. The scholarly and thoughtful Septimus was one of Lucius's oldest friends.

Lucius knew it had been two thousand years since Legio LIV entered the Somnum. Of course, Arminius and his barbarian hordes were long dead and turned to dust. But that did not stop him from pursuing the goal of avenging the dead. Now, only he and his tribunus laticlavius, or second in command, Marcus Titus, were left to remember those three savage days of slaughter and cruelty. The legion, or what remained of it, had resolutely followed Lucius from Gallicae, through Belgicae, and across the Rhenus Frontier into Germania. They marched into Germania hoping to find some kind of enemy fort or encampment that symbolized the hereditary descendants of Arminius's warriors. But Lucius would not attack or murder the innocent. He refused to stoop to the level of the savages that had killed thousands of men, women, and children, including Lucius's wife, Livia, and their little son, Cornelius. No, his enemies would be armed warriors.

Even with twenty centuries having passed, Lucius was determined to prove that Rome's legions never forgot, never forgave, and would never rest until they had their revenge.

But their invasion had not gone unnoticed. They were being hunted by men with strange flying craft and vehicles that moved without horses. With little choice, they trudged on, night after night, until they reached a pass in the mountains. The lead scout, Plutonius, had found a huge camp or festival beyond the mountains, but it was too far for the legion to reach without detection. It was then that Lucius chose to set up an ambush and attack on the road at the point where it cut through the mountain crest. It was a sort of poetic justice that Legio LIV would find its revenge in a deeply wooded forest along a road just as Arminius had done to Varus's army so long ago.

All through the morning, the legionaries had bent to their tasks with renewed vigor. They followed Lucius's orders quickly and without question. As the sun beat down on the laboring Romans, the parade of large and small vehicles roared past, oblivious to the danger in the thick woods. There had been one bad moment when a column of large vehicles came up the road. Lucius and Marcus were supervising the work by the road when one of the scouts signaled the alert. Ducking into the brush, the Romans watched as a line of twenty large machines drew closer with a sound like an avalanche. They were identical, painted a dark green with cloth roofs. The machines bore five-pointed white stars and black shields with a white eagle's head. Each vehicle carried at least twenty men dressed alike in clothing that was the color of the forest: green, tan, and brown.

Soldiers.

The machines roared past with whirlwinds of roiled dust and hot wind. Lucius could only watch in mute fury as they passed unmolested. For just an instant, he thought of ordering Regulus's archers to loose their arrows at the rushing machines, but it would have been foolish. Their trap was not yet ready. A moment after the last machine passed, the men of the legion resumed their preparations. Since then, the number of vehicles had dwindled to a trickle. There were long periods when none came roaring up the pass from either direction. But Lucius was certain the machines were going to the huge encampment he'd seen at dawn. They would be back. It made no difference to Lucius and Legio LIV if they caught the Germanic army going out or coming back. The result would be the same. Total annihilation.

As the last preparations were completed, Lucius and Marcus pulled on their armor and weapons. Lucius, tall and strongly built with dark brown intelligent eyes and the sharply defined features of his Italian blood, adjusted the gladius sword on his hip. The weapon had been in his hands when he used it to kill German barbarians on that bloody road. It had been hand-forged by Vulcanus, the finest blacksmith in the village of Orvieto, where Lucius had been born and raised. The smithy had given the young legionary the gladius on the day he completed his training.

Marcus Titus was a head taller than Lucius, built like a wrestler, and spoke in a voice that resounded like a battle drum. "All we need now is another of those long trains of green vehicles to come this way," he said.

"They will return, or more will come," Lucius said confidently. He put on his helmet. It gleamed in the late-morning sunlight. The faded red horsehair crest drooped but still proclaimed his rank as the legion's legatus. His armor, which had been weathered and rusty, was now nearly pristine and polished. All the legionaries were to look their best for the coming battle. They cut their hair, trimmed their beards, scoured their armor with granite dust from the local rock, and quickly washed their tunics in a nearby stream.

Just before the sun reached its zenith, Lucius called them together for a short speech. His surviving officers gathered the men not on watch. Close by was the burly and courageous Primus Ordanes of Cohort Jupiter, Marius Vitellus, the son of a slain officer in Legio XVIII. Next to him was the young Primus Ordanes of Cohort Apollo, Pompaeus Sestus, who lost two uncles to Arminius. Standing next to them were the inseparable brothers known as the "Three Stars," Regulus, Sirius, and Centaurus. To Lucius's left were his engineer, Arcturius, the stalwart Plutonius, and the powerful Marcus. Beyond them were the nearly five hundred legionaries who had followed him from Gallicae. Every man wore his armor and carried his weapons. This was the moment for which they had all lusted.

He smiled at them. "My brave and noble legionaries, this is the day we have waited for. Our cause is about to come to fruition. A long time has passed, and the world has forgotten us. But we have not, nor will we ever forget our duty to our fallen brothers so long ago in this very land of treachery and barbarity."

To a man, the legion stood straighter and watched their legatus with pride.

"We have traveled far, seen many of our friends and brothers fall, we have learned of the ages that have passed since we began the Somnum. Our families are long gone, Rome as we knew it might be a thing of the past, but we survivors of the greatest legion ever to follow the banners of Rome are here still. Forgotten we may be, but forgotten we will not remain. We are to show the world for all time what it is to be an enemy of Rome, of the Empire, and to soldiers of a Roman Legion. We may not see the sun set at day's end, but we will be with the gods as men who have earned their place in the stars."

The soldiers of Legio LIV Vindicta waved their swords and spears. Their armor and helmets flashed in the sunlight of their day of deliverance.

"Legionaries!" Lucius commanded. "Take your posts."

The soldiers moved off to take their positions along the road. "I wish Septimus could have been here to see this," Marcus said in a husky voice.

Lucius felt a wave of emotion fill his soul. "He is, Marcus. He is." Then he looked at the blue sky overhead. *Gods of our fathers, I only ask that you grant my loyal legion their victory. They have lost so much and given all they had for this chance. I beseech you, do not take this last hope from them. When it is over, they will rest at last in the company of their brothers and comrades.*

Lucius Cassius Aquilius's warrior heart quickened with the promise of battle, of revenge. His men were ready. All they needed was a target.

It had taken just over half an hour for the balky thermostat on the eleventh truck to cool down under Sergeant Haaber's patient gaze. He finally jumped down from the heavy bumper and pulled the hood down. "We're ready to go," he said as he and the driver closed the four latches on the hood. Then he wiped the grime from his hands with a cloth. "It should be fine now."

"No problem with the climb into the mountains?" Weber asked.

Haaber shook his head. "*Nein*. I reset the thermostat. I'll stay with this truck and keep an eye on the gauge."

Weber ran back up the line of trucks, calling out as he went. "All trucks mount up to move out!" When he reached Koll in the staff car, he looked back down the line. "We're ready to proceed."

"Excellent," Koll said. "Move out."

"We are just ahead of schedule," Weber said.

"I know," his commander replied, glancing at his watch. "I think it would be good to try and make up some time. I would still like to arrive early to give the men time to wash up before the parade."

Weber agreed. The column, having previously traveled at the maximum economic speed of seventy-five kilometers per hour, now accelerated until they zoomed along the smooth blacktop at nearly ninety. This made Koll feel better, and he once again began reviewing the things they'd have to do upon reaching the rally site.

A few kilometers ahead was the turnoff to the A60, followed by the climb to the pass.

Horst Molders clicked off his radio. "Observer Three reports the battalion is on the move again. Apparently, their mechanical problem has been repaired. Their speed is now ninety kilometers per hour."

"Good," Hauser said. His own column had had to slow down to keep from overtaking the army unit. "By my calculations, we are fifteen minutes behind them. How long will Observer Three be in trail?"

"He is breaking off the surveillance now," Molders replied. "The battalion is almost at the A60 turnoff. It is too risky for Observer Three to close in and maintain surveillance."

Hauser again looked at his watch. "Becker, slow down and keep your eyes open for them. We must not be seen."

"*Jawohl*," the driver said.

Molders called Kiel and Mannheim in the trailing staff car. "Panzer Two to Panzer Three. Speed now seven-five kph."

Hauser's own radio beeped for attention. "This is Panzer One," he said, using his code name. A voice came over the scrambled circuit. "Wolf here. What is your status?"

"We are approaching the A60 turnoff an estimated ten minutes behind the battalion," Hauser said. "We are back on schedule. Is there any change at your end?"

"Negative, Panzer One. The NATO officials and Hoffman's party have arrived."

Hauser felt a tingling in his spine at those words. "We will call at minus-thirty minutes."

"Very well, Panzer One. Wolf out."

Molders and Hauser permitted themselves a smile. In an hour, they'd arrive at the rally, ready and loaded. If all went well and his men performed exactly as they'd been trained, a new Germany would be born the next time the sun rose. The NOD leaders in Berlin were ready to take over the government as soon as Hauser reported the capture of Chancellor Hoffman and his staff. And Josef Hauser, poised at the Schwerpunkt of his troops, the leader of the first strike against the forces who were destroying his homeland with tainted foreign blood and inferior ideals, was ready. Ready for anything. He felt that tingle growing stronger, a quickening in his body.

At that moment, the 514 surviving officers and legionaries of Legio LIV Vindicta were hidden along both sides of the road just west of the highest pass through the ridgeline. Lucius was at the center of the line that stretched nearly three hundred paces along the road.

Next to him was the faithful aquilifer, Quintus, who had carried the legion's standard from Gallicae. Quintus once again held the staff bearing the eagle and imago of Augustus.

To Lucius's left was Vitellus, commanding Cohort Jupiter, while across the road, Marcus waited with Cohorts Mars and Apollo, the latter under the command of the loyal Sestus. The legion's eighty-eight surviving archers under the three brothers, Regulus, Sirius, and Centaurus, were arrayed in groups of five hidden on both sides of the road.

Lucius watched for the signal from Plutonius's scouts. When it came, their long wait for revenge would be over.

At the head of the speeding Gebirgsjäger column, Sergeant Dorfman glared at the GPS unit on the staff car's dashboard. For the first time since he'd begun using it, the unit was failing him. Driving northeast on the B45, he waited for the electronic voice to signal the impending junction with the A60. But for the last two hours, the GPS had worked only intermittently.

Dorfman reached out his right hand to hit the "Recalculate" button. It was tiny, and he had to feel for it. With his eyes trying to look in two places at once, he missed the exit, and the sedan swept past the turnoff. The column rolled over the bridge above the A60 and continued on.

The radio chirped for attention. "Staff, this is Sergeant Rittman in Truck 14. We missed the A60 turnoff. Please clarify. Over."

Dorfman's eyes shot to the dashboard, but the GPS didn't make a sound. Then he saw a road sign pass on his left and read the reversed wording in his side mirror: *Verzweigung A60 2 km.*

Koll, who was in a conversation with Weber in the back seat, said, "What was that call, Dorfman? I did not hear what it said."

The veteran sergeant didn't make any excuses. "I'm sorry, Colonel, I missed the turn. We have to turn around."

Koll nodded. "Weber, call the trucks. We'll do a turnabout as soon as we can find room." He didn't berate the contrite sergeant. He was too good a commander for that. "We are still ahead of schedule."

Ten minutes later, Dorfman saw a wide turnout on the right, and Weber made a call to the trucks. "Turnout on the right. Slow and execute a single-line turn. Watch for traffic."

Soon the nineteen Gebirgsjäger vehicles had made the turn and were headed back to the turnoff to the A60. Koll estimated they had lost about fifteen minutes. They could make that up once they had made it through the pass. Behind the staff car, the seventeen heavy trucks and trailing staff car followed.

"For God's sake! What is the driver trying to do?" Helmut said as he held the post that supported the canvas cover. "Trying out for roller coaster operator?" As the truck leaned into another sweeping turn, he had to use both hands to keep from being thrown into the man across from him.

"We're trying to make up time," said Walther, who held the heavy framework against the cab. "That wrong turn could delay us, and Colonel Koll wants to get to the rally early. We're well into the Westerwald on the A60. We'll be at the top of the pass in a few minutes."

"I hope so," Helmut said. "That lunch we had at Limburg is deciding whether to come back up."

"Try and hold on," Walther replied. He felt a little queasy too. "We want time to hit the latrines and clean up before we assemble as Chancellor Hoffman's honor guard."

"It wouldn't do to vomit during Hoffman's speech," Corporal Kranz said with a loud belch. "Damn that meat stew."

"Did you have to say that?" another soldier moaned. They were pressed to the right as the truck rounded another curve. The driver shifted gears as they climbed farther into the mountains. The tires squealed as Helmut felt the immense inertia of the truck's body leaning out. He looked out the open rear of the truck bed. "We're leaving a lot of rubber on the road," he observed.

In the lead staff car, Koll's watch read 1202 hours. They were due to arrive at 1300. It was at least five more kilometers to the pass. Once through, they'd begin the descent through the foothills to the park. They were almost there. He saw blue sky far ahead when the BMW swept around one wide turn. The trees were still thick, but he saw some open clearings as they climbed toward the pass.

Dorfman was now following Weber's directions and petulantly ignoring the chattering GPS. He was determined to get Gebirgsjäger Battalion 232 to the rally ahead of schedule, even if he had to break more than a few local traffic laws.

The A60 wound its way uphill into the Rothaar Mountains. Along the road were wide shoulders for bicycles and hikers. Hauser could see only a short way into the dense trees on either side. The thick forest seemed to swallow light, turning the distance into dark green moiré patterns of mottled light and shadow. Becker downshifted as they came to a steeper rise, and Hauser felt himself lurch forward. He checked his watch for the hundredth time. "I wish there were some way to know that we were behind the army column," he said.

"We are," Molders said confidently as he pointed at the road ahead. "See those tire marks?"

Hauser squinted and saw black streaks on the clean road surface, like brush strokes painted by a colorblind artist. "Yes, I see them."

"Those were made by a military convoy. Their trucks are heavy and lose a great deal of rubber on turns like this. Most vehicles don't leave any at all. I saw them only after we turned onto the A60. They are definitely ahead of us. We can close the interval after we are through the pass."

That satisfied Hauser, and he once again went through the mental checklist for the operation.

Far to the rear in the trailing staff car, Mathias Kiel and Anton Mannheim, both wearing the uniforms of Gebirgsjäger Battalion 232 lieutenants, watched the rear of the last truck in the column moving up the winding motorway. "I will be glad when we get there," Mannheim said as his stomach gave a queasy lurch. "I left the army because I hated long road marches. Look at me now."

Kiel, whose time in the Bundeswehr had spanned more than two decades, smiled. "It will not be long now." He turned to look out the rear window. They were just cresting a rise, and he could see for many kilometers. For just an instant, he thought he saw the olive drab canvas

of at least three army trucks in the distance. But all of the NOD's trucks
were ahead. He pondered it briefly but was interrupted by a call from
Molders to reduce speed to sixty kph. He gave the order to the driver and
resumed reviewing his job once they reached the rally.

CHAPTER III

THE DEADLY FOREST

The legion's trap was ready to be sprung on the Germans. Lucius's heart pounded with excitement and a lust for revenge. *Two thousand years we have waited,* he thought as a single red vehicle sped up the road past him. *Septimus Deo is watching over us, as is Titus Clavius, Drusus Vitellus, Dominitus Severus, Marius Civilus, and all the others. I only hope that the cursed spirit of Arminius is watching from the underworld to see what we are about to do to his people. Watch, Arminius, you will soon have much company.* The thought made him smile.

Legio LIV Vindicta was ready to kill.

Colonel Koll's ears finally popped as Dorfman shifted the BMW into low gear a few kilometers from the pass. He sighed, glad the interminable winding road was nearly over. It would be a smooth ride to the plains beyond the pass.

"Sire! The signal!"

Lucius snapped his head to the right as a legionary pointed down the slope along the road. An arrow arced down from the treetops and speared its way into the ground less than twenty paces from him. The arrow had a strip of red tied above the fletching.

Every man along both sides of the road saw it streak over them. They readied their bows, swords, and spears. The time for battle was upon them.

Over the pounding of his heart, Lucius heard the sound of many approaching vehicles. The noise grew into the familiar roar that accompanied the big green machines. From a curve far down the road, a single green vehicle appeared. Behind it was the first of a long line of large machines like the ones that had passed earlier. They were driving right into the Roman trap. Then Lucius heard the rapid thumping of axes on wood. Their trap was about to be sprung.

He waved at Marcus, fifty paces away on the far side of the road. Lucius easily read the fierce light of victory in his friend's dark eyes.

The staff car slowed when Dorfman took a particularly sharp turn. Koll leaned to absorb the motion. He looked out the window and saw a man in the brush. The man was wearing something shiny . . . metal? Armor? No, it was probably a bicyclist wearing garish red and silver biking togs. Koll forgot about it and waited for the car to stop swaying. The column of heavy trucks slowed in the turn.

The sharp tearing sound of splintering wood signaled the first tall evergreen falling in a slow arc as the long slender trunk dropped across the road with the cracks of snapping branches. A moment later another tree fell, then a third. Arcturius's engineers had done well, cutting the trunks with their sharp axes until only enough wood remained to keep the trees standing. On seeing the signal, they chopped the last bit to allow the tall pines to drop exactly in place. The road at the crest of the pass was completely blocked. The first machine would reach the barrier in a few more seconds. Lucius turned to look down the road beyond the vehicles passing his position. He could not see the far end of the line. They were almost all in the trap now.

"Goddamn!" Dorfman slammed down on the brakes. The staff car ˙''˙ₑ it was on ice, throwing Koll and Weber off-balance.

"What is it?" Koll's first thought was of the heavy trucks just behind the stopped car. Then he heard the hiss of air brakes and squealing tires.

"What the hell?" Dorfman growled. "How did those get there?" He pointed ahead. "Trees, Colonel. Fallen on the road."

The officers leaned forward and saw the long brown and green foliage of the pines lying directly across their path. Koll turned to Weber. "Quick! Call the trucks. Tell them to stop. We don't want them to bunch up or hit one another."

The sound of the truck's engine changed pitch, then lessened to a vibrating idle. The brakes hissed and the truck came to a stop.

"What is going on now?" Helmut said. "First the broken radiator, then the wrong turn. We're never going to get there at this rate."

Walther leaned into the cab. He heard what sounded like Weber's voice on the radio.

"Something about a fallen tree blocking the road."

"Our luck hasn't changed," Helmut said. He lifted the canvas cover and peered out at the forest beyond the side of the road. "Nice out there," he said.

It was time. The vehicles had all stopped. Lucius signaled to Marcus, who brought his voice from the deepest part of his huge body. "Archers!" The stentorian bellow echoed through the forest. All down the road, Regulus's eighty-eight surviving archers had already nocked their arrows. As one, they stood and raised their recurved bows and aimed at the big green vehicles. Some aimed at the men in the front cabs visible through open windows.

"Loose!" Marcus yelled. With a single loud thrumming noise, nearly ninety bowstrings propelled the iron-tipped arrows point-blank into the thin canvas sides of the trucks.

In the cab of the lead truck, the driver didn't even have time to shout before an arrow drove itself through his skull. He collapsed onto the man next to him, who died almost instantly from an arrow from the other side. One truck veered out of control as the dying driver slumped against the wheel. The heavy green truck plowed into the brush, crushing a pair of Romans who could not react in time.

The thick green canvas was no protection as the sharp arrowheads scythed through and immediately caused carnage among the men inside, who had no warning. Dozens were killed instantly by the deadly fusillade of arrows stabbing into their backs. Seconds later, the next flight was loosed, then a third. Dozens more were killed or maimed inside the trucks. Rivers of blood pooled and ran across the wooden truck beds as they were transformed into metal coffins.

It was a slaughter.

"What the hell are those trees doing across the road?" Hauser growled as the staff car lurched to a stop just short of the pass.

"I'll find out, Josef." Horst Molders was just opening the passenger door when the archers released their first deadly attack. Becker fell against the door with an arrow embedded in his left eye.

A trained soldier, Molders reacted immediately, ducking below the window and grabbing the radio off the seat. "Alert all Tigers! This is Panzer Two! We're under attack! Get your men out and fight back!"

In the backseat, Hauser was too stunned to grasp the sudden assault. He heard Molders's orders, but they meant nothing to him. "What is happening?"

Molders used the door as a shield. "Keep your head down, Josef! Someone is shooting at us from the woods!"

Hauser ducked his head. There was no gunfire. "Who—" he started to say, but a sharp hissing sound passed his left ear through the open window. There was a shriek of pain, and Molders fell from the car with an arrow shaft in his neck.

"Shit!" Hauser gasped. The air was filled with the humming and tearing of hundreds of arrows spearing past and into the column. For all his zeal and passion as a revolutionary, Josef Hauser was no soldier. He was completely unprepared to deal with what was happening around him. Even as the leader of the paramilitary arm of the NOD, he'd received only moderate training in the use of weapons. His best military advisor was lying dead only a few feet away. Hauser cowered behind the door. He heard a loud *thump*! To his horror, he saw the point of an arrow protruding from the inner door panel. He yelled for help. But none would be coming from his men. Then he remembered his pistol and pulled it out of the holster. He held the weapon to his chest as scant protection from the disaster around him.

"Get out!" a sergeant in one of the trucks yelled. "Get out and take cover! We're going to get killed if we stay in here!" The NOD terrorists who had survived the first volleys snatched up their assault rifles and scrambled out of the still-idling trucks. Several fell at once from arrows and lay writhing on the asphalt. They sought cover beneath the vibrating hot steel and looked for the attackers. The next volley of arrows came in low to strike the men huddled under the vehicles. Men were killed instantly when arrows pierced the top of their heads.

"Fire, damn you!" yelled a platoon leader. "Kill them!" Reacting using the training they'd received over months of preparation, the first NOD terrorists returned fire. The modern assault rifles quickly took a toll on the Romans, the 5.56mm bullets cutting down the armored men as they stood to loose arrows or throw spears. But the Roman legionaries continued to attack and slaughter the Germans. The strangest battle in the history of warfare started in the deep forest of Central Germany.

Three minutes after the first volley, more than a third of Hauser's men were dead. They hung like rag dolls from the cabs and backs of the trucks, with arrows sprouting from them like stiff grass. All down the entire column, the would-be revolutionaries of the New Order of Deutschland desperately fought back or looked for an escape. But every direction they turned led only to more death.

In the trailing staff car, Kiel and Mannheim saw the trucks ahead swerving from the sudden onslaught. The air hummed with the sound of arrows and screaming men. Bodies fell from the last truck, with blood dripping in scarlet rivulets onto the black roadway.

"Turn around!" Mannheim yelled at the driver. "Get us out of here!"

Shaking with fear, the driver managed to turn around and head down the road. He saw the way blocked by several dozen Romans running at them, carrying spears, axes, and swords. He veered to avoid them but lost control and crashed into the heavy brush on the side of the road. The Romans leapt on him and the two NOD officers, killing them at once. The attackers had just finished the job of felling the trees to block any escape back down the road to the west. Once the Germans were dead, they ran up the hill to join the battle.

Lieutenant Colonel Koll was walking uphill toward the fallen trees blocking the road when the first rattle of automatic weapons fire echoed from ahead. "Who is firing?" Koll said as he spun around, trying to localize the noise. "It sounds like a damned battle! Those felled trees have to be connected somehow." Then his eyes went wide. "The Americans!"

Weber stared at him in horror. "Some lunatic anti-NATO fanatics are attacking the American troops. They're unarmed!"

Koll grabbed his radio and snapped out a stream of orders. "Bentele! Tell Lieutenant Essen to issue the ammunition. Full bandoliers. Full field packs for the medics. Move!" He said to his aid, "Weber, get on the radio to the command post at the rally. Get some help up here while I get the troops moving."

He ran down the line of trucks, shouting orders as he went. "Fall in! Grab your weapons! Draw ammo at the last truck! Wulff, Klausmeyer, Haaber, get your squads moving!"

More gunfire reverberated down the road.

Back at the head of the column, Weber was in contact with the command post at the rally. "This is 232 Battalion! I need to talk to someone in command. There's a damned battle being fought up here!"

Lucius was at the center of Cohort Jupiter, moving up and down the line of legionaries. He watched the attack with the eye of a veteran, telling Centaurus where to direct the archers' arrows. He was consumed with an elation he'd never before known. His very heart and body were charged with wild excitement. His men rained death and revenge on the Germanic descendants of Arminius and his treacherous countrymen. Centaurus's skilled archers loosed deadly arrows into the cloth sides of the vehicles. Green-clad men scrambled out and ran into the woods only ˙ ' ˙ legionaries waiting with their spears and swords. None made it more than a few steps, falling with ghastly wounds spilling blood into the soil of their homeland.

Lucius saw that they used the same sort of fire-hammers he'd seen in the hands of the lawmen two weeks ago. Long flashes of yellow fire spat from them with the sound of lightning. The enemy cut down a dozen legionaries before they could get close enough to attack. A German fired at Centaurus just as he loosed an arrow at the same man. They died at the same moment. Then the loyal, eager Sestus fell into a twitching heap with several black holes torn in his armor. But he had already killed five of the Germans.

At that moment, Lucius felt a sudden hot shock on his shoulder that spun him to the ground. Gasping, he rolled over. It seemed as if his entire upper body had been doused in hot lava. A legionary scuttled over to him. "Sire! You are hit!"

Lucius shook his head, trying to clear it. Then he looked at his left shoulder. The overlapping armor plates were torn open, and a thin stream of bright red blood oozed from a tear in his flesh. "It is nothing, legionary," he said, gritting his teeth. "Return to your duty."

The man hesitated only for a moment, then picked up his weapons and resumed fighting. Pulling a piece of cloth from his haversack, Lucius shoved it into the jagged rent in the armor. The wound was deep but he could still move his left arm. With a grunt of pain, he rose to his feet and continued to direct the battle.

Marcus witnessed this but never ceased his duties. When he saw Lucius standing, he roared, "Regulus! Tell your archers to concentrate on the men under the machines. The ones with the fire-hammers! Those with gladii and pila, concentrate on the cowards who are running!"

"Aye, Sire!" Regulus was furious at the death of his brother Centaurus and the injury to his Legatus. "Sirius! Tell your archers to seek out the men under the vehicles! Kill them where they lay! If you are out of arrows, use your pila!" With that, more than fifty men charged out of the woods and ran directly at the men huddled under the line of idling trucks. In seconds the sounds of desperate hand-to-hand combat filled the forest. Grunts and screams, gunfire and the thud of metal on flesh filled the air all along the road. The skilled and experienced veteran

Roman legionaries with arrows, swords, and spears were pitted against an outnumbered enemy armed with assault rifles. Death quickly cut down men on both sides.

Lucius saw one of Plutonius's scouts, long hair flapping wildly from under his helmet, run for the nearest vehicle with his gladius out. He dived under it and singlehandedly killed two men cowering there, stabbing them in the throat. Another German fired point-blank at him, and the scout was torn open as he fell in a spray of blood.

A banshee yell made Lucius snap his head around to see the burly Vitellus charging out of the brush with a pilum in one hand and his gladius in the other. "Come out you cowardly sons of diseased whores! Come out and feel the vengeance of Rome! I am here to avenge my great father, Drusus Vitellus of Legio Eighteen!" He waved his bloody gladius. "Follow me, my legionaries!"

A score of Romans erupted from the trees to join the enraged Vitellus. Their mad rush overwhelmed the Germans under four of the vehicles as they were dragged out and butchered. Vitellus laughed maniacally as he stabbed three of the enemy with his weapons. As each one fell, he screamed into the sky. "Father, I avenge your murder!"

A German who had taken cover behind one of the big wheels managed to get his weapon up and fired. Two of Vitellus's men fell, but the veteran shoved the barbed spear into the man's open mouth. The bloody point exploded from the back of his skull. Then another burst of hot death finally cut down the brave Vitellus. When he fell, Lucius clearly saw a look of triumph on his gore-streaked face. He died exactly as his father had, with weapons in his hands.

Vitellus's brave charge emboldened more legionaries who ran forward and thrust their own pila into the few Germans still resisting. A few tried to run but quickly fell from the spear points and blades.

A pride worthy of a Caesar welled up in Lucius's breast. He ran across the road and joined Marcus. "The gods are with us!"

"What a glorious victory, Lucius Cassius!" yelled the big man as he nearly decapitated a fleeing German with a savage swipe of his sword. "Tell Arminius to boil in the River Styx, pig!"

The two Roman officers ran up and down the lines of howling legionaries, exhorting them to kill, kill, and kill again.

Only ten minutes had elapsed since the trees fell to the road. More than two hundred and seventy members of the enemy were dead or fatally wounded.

But most of Legio LIV's legionaries and officers had also fallen in the desperate battle.

CHAPTER IV

RED WITH GERMAN BLOOD

The emergency call from Captain Weber caused immediate chaos and confusion at the park administration headquarters. The dispatchers in the communications room were suddenly the center of attention as three park officials tried to understand what was happening up in the mountains and what to do. They were completely out of their element in such a situation. They could not divert any of the park security or local police. Their job was to protect the thousands of people *inside* the park.

Then one official suddenly recalled who was coordinating security operations outside the park. "Call the Landespolizei command post! Relay those calls to them!"

In moments, Weber's frantic transmissions were routed to the trailer at the park's western boundary.

The sudden revelation that a battle was unfolding in the mountains caused an immediate reaction among the people in the Landespolizei command trailer. A female dispatcher was on the radio talking to Weber while Ortmann barked orders to her response teams.

At that moment, Braden entered the trailer, followed by Morley, Sharon, and Rabble. Braden was about to ask what was happening when he heard a voice on the radio. "I repeat, send some armed men up to the pass! We need armed backup!"

Ortmann was standing by the dispatcher. "Call the response squad and prepare them to move up the A60. Make sure they are fully armed with riot gear. Find out who is shooting at whom." She turned and saw the four of them standing by the door.

"It seems you were right, Herr Braden," she said. "Someone is fighting a battle up on the road." She turned to the woman who was on the radio. "What was that last thing he said?"

"The Gebirgsjäger officer says that someone is attacking the American unit," said the woman.

"No," Ortmann said. "The American 101st arrived safely almost an hour ago. They are in their staging area. General Worden left half an hour ago to meet them."

It was then that Braden noted the absence of the tall German officer. "Can you reach him?"

Ortmann was about to reply when the dispatcher turned to her. "The patrol at the west gate is calling in. They report faint gunfire coming from the mountains."

Ortmann grabbed the handset. "This is Ortmann. Repeat that."

The voice of Rudolf Bach came over the speaker. "Colonel, the wind is blowing from the west. Very faint, but there is no mistaking it. Automatic weapons fire."

"Bach," Ortmann said, "the response team is on the way. Have your squad join them when they reach the gate. Full riot gear and weapons."

"Understood, Colonel," Bach replied. "What are our orders when we reach the site?"

"Be on the alert, report what you see, and if possible, get control of the situation. Friendlies coming up the road from the west. Be careful. Over."

"Copy that," Bach replied. "We will move out as soon as the response team arrives. Over."

Schroeder charged into the trailer. "I just heard on my radio," he said breathlessly. "232 Battalion is under attack?" He was almost shaking with anger.

"No, they are not," Ortmann said. "They reported gunfire on the road ahead of them. We're sending the response team and the west gate squad up the A60 to investigate and report. That's about sixty armed men."

Schroeder looked around the trailer. "Where in the hell is Worden?"

"At the rally," Ortmann said without turning from the radio. "I sent a runner to find him. He is not responding to our calls."

The Landespolizei commissioner rolled his eyes at the ceiling. "He is off kissing the asses of the NATO brass and politicians!"

"We will find him later," Ortmann said, still trying to get control of the situation. "We don't need him right now."

While the Germans were talking, Braden turned to Rabble and the others. "If the 101st is already here and the Gebirgsjäger isn't involved, then who's doing the shooting? And who are they shooting at?"

Sharon and Morley could only shake their heads in mute shock.

"I don't know," Rabble said, glancing out the windows to the west. "But one thing is certain. Someone is up there on the pass shooting at someone else. And I bet Lucius is right in the thick of it."

Ortmann was talking to Weber again. "Captain, can you see anything? Who is fighting who? Over." Ortmann held her breath.

"We can't see far enough up the road to see anyone. There are fallen trees blocking the road. Colonel Koll is heading up there right now with one company. Over."

The popping sound of distant machine gun fire rippled from the speaker.

Schroeder blurted, "They are unarmed!"

That did it. Braden spun on his heels and ran for the door. Right behind him were Morley, Sharon, and Rabble.

Ortmann called out, "Where are you going?"

"I'm going with the response team," Braden said, pulling the door open. "I have to be there."

"I can't allow that. You're civilians."

"I am a NATO criminal investigator. So is Rabble. Professor Morley and Doctor Kelly are part of the team. We have to be there."

He had no authority and even less of a logical reason for going, but the expression on his face left no doubt he meant every word. Then he looked at Ann and felt a sudden mix of emotions. He wanted her to be with him but also feared for her safety. "Ann, I think you'd better stay here."

Her determined expression surprised him. "Not on your life, love. I'm a qualified paramedic, remember? You might need me. I'm going."

For just a second, he considered refusing, but her logic and resolve won over. "Okay. But you stay out of the way. I'm sure the police have emergency medical packs."

Ortmann nodded. "Follow Captain Bach's orders. Do you understand?"

"I do," Braden said as he ran out the door, followed by the others.

Schroeder also turned for the door. "Call Bach and have them wait for us." With a muttered curse, he left the trailer.

The battle was almost over. All but a few of the Germans were dead from arrows, spears, or swords. Legionaries climbed into the big vehicles to find and kill the few remaining survivors. Many Germans begged and cried for their lives, but there was no mercy. The legion had waited too long and sacrificed too much to show any pity.

There were stretches along the curving road where Lucius found only dead men. Everywhere he looked, dozens of his loyal legionaries had fallen. Their bodies were torn or smashed by the horrifying German fire-hammers. The road was a river of blood. It reminded Lucius of the bloody road in the forest so long ago.

The fighting continued sporadically. When a Roman fell to a German, there was always another to take his place. Lucius saw Plutonius, the faithful scout, lying in a heap with a dozen bloody holes in his armor. Next to his crimson-streaked gladius were the bodies of three Germans. Lucius felt no remorse for the dead Germans. These were soldiers, military men, who knew the risks and dangers of life under arms for their country. But most of the men in the mottled green and brown clothes acted more like the barbarians of Arminius's horde than professional soldiers. Some had run like cowards, shrieking and crying, leaving their comrades behind. Only a few Germans still resisted. They had managed to find good cover under the vehicles, and every attempt to reach them failed. Of all the enemy soldiers his legion was fighting, these men merited respect.

By the time Lucius reached the last vehicle, he had counted less than sixty surviving legionaries and only two officers, besides himself and Marcus. Time was running out. They would have to leave very soon.

It had been only fifteen minutes since the trees had stopped the NOD column. And in that short time, Josef Hauser had cowered and watched as his dream, his planning, his hopes and ambitions for a new Germany were torn to shreds by a merciless enemy with primitive weapons. His last remaining men were being massacred one by one. Every time one of his men tried to fire his rifle, archers and men with spears pinpointed the assaulter.

And they never missed.

The screams of men and moans of the dying drowned out the diminishing rifle fire. He realized it was only a matter of time before all his men died. The New Order of Deutschland had died a horrible and totally impossible death before their finest hour. Who were these armored fiends who had attacked them? Why had they done it? Josef Hauser did not know. Out of sheer luck, he was still alive, huddling behind the door of his staff car. He saw no escape. Sooner or later, the wild demons would find and butcher him. He was both frightened and angry.

Lucius Cassius Aquilius had finally fulfilled his duty and restored the honor of the Roman Army. Legio LIV had fully and honorably avenged the murder of Varus's legions in the deadly forest. He felt at peace even among the death his men savagely wreaked on the Germans. Then he remembered something. He was thinking of a day long ago, a hillside over a road covered in gore and dead men. In his mind's eye, he saw a trio of German tribal chieftains shouting an order. An order to stop the killing. He made a decision and trotted back up the line to where Marcus was walking among the dead and dying. Blood and gore splattered his big body and armor, and his swarthy face was streaked with sweat and dirt. But his eyes held only elation. "Lucius Cassius," the big man yelled in triumph. "We are victorious."

Hauser heard the shout. He watched two Romans wearing ornate armor and helmets with bedraggled crests talking. The shorter one said something to the other, who was taller and appeared to be in command. *An officer.* Hauser felt the weight of the Walther pistol in his hand. Thirsting for some sort of revenge, he slowly raised the pistol until it came over the lower edge of the window frame and sighted down the barrel. He waited for his opportunity. He could not miss.

"Marcus," Lucius said, catching his breath, "it is time to stop the killing. Those few Germans still alive have earned their right to survive. I think you know why."

The big man peered at his friend for a moment. Then he nodded. "Yes, I do. We have killed enough. A few should survive to tell the tale of our long-awaited vengeance." He waved his sword over his head. "Legionaries!" he bellowed. "By order of your legatus, you will stop the fighting! Pass the word to regroup here." Turning to Lucius, the giant smiled from a face dripping with sweat. "We await your orders."

The loud bark of a fire-hammer shattered the near-silence. Marcus's face contorted in agony as he was driven back by a powerful blow. His eyes were wide in surprise as he fell at Lucius's feet. A stream of blood poured from the big man's chest and pooled on the ground.

It had happened in three terrible seconds. Lucius looked with horror as his old friend, the strongest man he had ever known, dropped like a sack of grain.

A legionary ran past them holding his gladius over his head. Another loud bang rang out, then a third. The Roman staggered momentarily but continued to run at the smaller green vehicle at the head of the column. Reaching into the open window, he grabbed the collar of a man screaming in terror. The enraged legionary savagely shoved the point of his sword into the man's ribs. The German dropped his weapon as he tried desperately to lift himself off the blade cutting into his heart. Blood spurted from the wound, staining his green uniform. He wilted and fell backward into the vehicle.

Lucius knelt at his friend's side and took his hand. Marcus was still alive but barely breathing. His eyes were open.

"Marcus," Lucius said in a thick voice, "I want to thank you. Thank you for your loyalty and your service. You will always be my closest and most devoted friend."

Marcus nodded weakly and spoke in a whisper. "Thank you, Lucius Cassius. I will be waiting for you in the sky." Then the strong heart stopped, and Marcus Titus was dead.

Lucius felt a heavy weight on his chest. They were all dead. Vitellus, Sestus, Plutonius, and Septimus. And now his most stalwart comrade, the mighty Marcus. He was the only survivor of Varus's slain legions. He stood and saw the remaining legionaries running up the hill toward them, led by Remus Draconius, a centurio in Sestus's Cohort Apollo. "Sire, there are men with more fire-hammers coming from below. I counted almost two full centuria of them."

"We must be gone from this place," Lucius said. "Assemble the survivors and prepare to march out." He did a fast head count. Legio LIV was down to forty-six men, and at least fifteen were wounded but able to walk. They would have to.

One of the walking wounded was the aquilifer, Quintus. He was weeping, not from the pain of a bloody wound in his stomach, but because of the object he cradled in his shaking hands. "Sire," he said in a voice of pure anguish, "I have failed you and our legion. I can never atone for this shame."

Lucius saw that Quintus was holding the shattered remains of the gold eagle and imago standard. "It was destroyed by a barbarian weapon." Quintus looked down at the fragments of gold-leafed wood. "I killed him with my bare hands, but I could not save the sacred aquilia."

Lucius showed the man a sad smile. "Quintus, you have not shamed us. *You* carried it from Rome to Gallicae and from Belgicae to here. I am proud of you."

The man sniffed and nodded. But before he could say anything else, he faltered and fell. The fragments lay scattered at his dead feet.

With a sigh, Lucius turned to Draconius. "Time is short." He knew where to go. It was the only place. But could they reach it? Could they survive the week it would take to find their final resting place? He did not know. But in the end, what did it matter? They'd done their duty, and honor had been restored. Whether they lived another week, another day, or another hour, the job had been done, and he was grateful to the gods for the gift.

"Move out," he ordered, seeing the last legionaries watching him. To a man, they showed pride on their haggard and bloody faces.

With faltering steps and dripping blood, but with a fire in their hearts, they left the road and disappeared into the dark forest, heading north.

Colonel Koll led his men up the road past the fallen trees. It was clear for a hundred meters to where it curved to the right. The two hundred men were moving in mutually supporting lines of a hundred men each. On the right was Major Bentele, while Lieutenant Otto Altmeyer led the left column.

Koll silently blessed his foresight to bring live ammunition despite orders. They advanced slowly with their weapons raised. There were armed men somewhere ahead. But there was only silence. Then just past the curve, Altmeyer found the first vehicle. It was a German Army BMW staff car in a shallow ditch off the road. Koll noted the open doors and approached with his pistol drawn. When he looked inside the vehicle, he saw blood and bodies. "Medics!" he yelled.

A corporal carrying a shoulder bag rushed over and began examining the bodies inside. He stood up a moment later. "All dead, Colonel. From massive penetrating trauma. Knives or bayonets, I suppose."

Koll didn't know what to think. He still had to find out what was happening. "Very well," he said. "Let's move on."

Private Helmut Schroeder, a few paces behind Altmeyer and Sergeant Wulff, was more alert than he'd ever been in training.

"What is going on?" Corporal Ernst Walther whispered. "Did you see that staff car? Full of dead men."

Helmut didn't reply. His senses were tuned to the silent black forest and the eerily empty road. Suddenly, they heard a single shot in the distance. "Down!" Altmeyer said as Bentele did the same on the other side of the road. But for a long moment, there was only the whisper of the wind in the trees. Then another shot rang out, followed by a third. The German soldiers knelt in the roadside ditches for a full minute, watching and waiting. But nothing else happened.

Koll stood and waved for them to continue. They slowly advanced up the winding motorway. Helmut felt a cool breeze fan his cheek from ahead. It carried a strange mix of scents. Diesel exhaust and . . . something else. It made his nose twitch. It was familiar, but he could not quite place it. Blood? This chilling thought was erased when his ears picked up the sound of running engines.

Then Altmeyer, forty paces ahead, called, "Colonel, there are trucks ahead."

Koll ran over to the younger officer. He looked to where Altmeyer was pointing. He saw army trucks, five of them. Beyond them, the road bent to the left, obscuring anything more.

"They are stopped," Koll observed, "but not parked. I see exhaust from the last one."

He waved for Sergeant Wulff to take his squad up the road and examine the trucks. "We will cover you from here," Koll said.

The veteran sergeant motioned for his men to follow. They moved closer to the idling trucks with their rifles at the ready. Wulff bent over under the nearest truck. He stood and turned toward Koll. His face was ashen. "Colonel! They are Bundeswehr troops!"

Koll ran over to the truck. It was stopped against a tree on the left side of the road. Under it were several more bodies. All were clearly dead, from . . . "Arrows?" He stood staring at the bizarre sight of men dressed in German uniforms, with dozens of arrow shafts protruding from their shoulders and heads. The asphalt under the truck was a sea of blood and gore. They held standard issue Heckler & Koch G36 rifles in frozen hands, and hundreds of spent casings were scattered all over. Koll bent down and felt the wrist of the nearest man. "Still warm. Some may still be alive. Check them all." While his officers and sergeants began examining the bodies, the soldiers kept alert for any danger. Koll keyed his radio. "Weber. Have all the medics head up this way. And call security at the rally to send ambulances, paramedics, everything. We have dead Bundeswehr troops up here." Then he had another thought. "And tell Lieutenant Schulz to take four men and the second staff car back to the junction of the B45 and set up a roadblock. We can't have any traffic coming up here."

"I already did that," Weber replied. "We stopped three vehicles and ordered them to turn around. They were not happy."

"Good work. You are in command until I get back."

"What should they say to any inquiries?"

"Tell them to detour to the old B45 route. And tell the gate at the rally to do the same. We don't dare let any civilians see what happened here."

"I'll call them right now. Weber out."

Koll watched his men searching the trucks, but so far, no one called for a medic. That meant there were no survivors. What in the hell had happened?

"Colonel," Weber said on the radio, "a response team is on the way from the rally. And they are putting up roadblocks. But they asked to confirm that the bodies are of Bundeswehr troops. Over."

"Affirmative," Koll said firmly. "No doubt." He went back to the trucks. His men were moving up the road.

"Colonel Koll!" yelled a soldier bent down by the next truck. "We've got some wounded! Get a medic up here!" Koll followed the medic to where the soldier was hunched over a man on the ground. He was grievously wounded by an arrow in his shoulder but alive. He was moaning nonsensically.

"Do what you can for him," Koll told the medic. "Ambulances will be here shortly."

Corporal Walther stood on the rear bumper and peered into the truck's load bed. He reeled in shock. "God! There are at least ten more bodies in here."

Koll and Altmeyer came over and looked into the charnel of the truck. On the floor and benches were more bodies bristling with arrows. Their blood covered the floor. Koll saw dozens of small slits in the canvas sides, the sun glinting through like golden diamonds. In the cab, the driver lay sideways on the seat, an arrow sticking straight through his head. Walther reached in and turned off the engine. The silence was deafening.

Koll was dumbfounded. "Who the hell did this? And who are these men?" Then he looked at one of the bodies on the ground. On the left shoulder was an Edelweiss patch. Instinctively, he glanced at his own shoulder and saw the identical patch. *What the hell?*

"They're Gebirgsjäger troops!" Helmut Schroeder said. "They're us! I mean . . ." He stopped, unable to voice his amazement.

"That is not possible," Koll said. "No other Gebirgsjäger battalion was ordered to be at the rally." He frowned, leaning on the truck's high bumper. Then he looked at the bumper. Painted on the green metal was the alphanumeric designation: GbJ Btn 232. Koll was leaning on a Gebirgsjäger Battalion 232 truck. "What is going on here?" he said to no one in particular. He pulled the radio from his belt. "Weber. Find out if any other Gebirgsjäger battalions were ordered to attend the rally."

Bentele was looking at the markings. "They're ours."

"Yes, apparently," Koll said. The radio chirped and he held it up. "Koll."

"Weber here. No other Gebirgsjäger or Bundeswehr units were to attend the rally, nor are there any in the region. All Gebirgsjäger are at their posts at this time. Gebirgsjäger 230 is on mountain maneuvers in eastern Bavaria. Over."

"Understood. Koll out." Understood? That was as close to a lie as anything he'd ever said in his life. They continued up the line of stalled and stopped trucks. Each told the same gory tale. Every truck held dead men and blood, and around them were more bodies on the road.

Bentele conferred with Altmeyer, then walked over to Koll. "We cannot find any identification on any of the bodies. No tags or wallets. Nothing."

Koll considered this. A thought popped into his mind. Impostors. The men were not real Bundeswehr troops.

He was turning to Bentele when he heard another shout. "Colonel! You must come and see this!"

"What now?" Koll said rhetorically and walked into the edge of the forest to where several soldiers were standing, pointing at the ground. "More Gebirgsjäger troops?"

"No, Colonel," said the soldier, whom he recognized as Helmut Schroeder. Koll bent to look. He dropped the radio in surprise. "What the—"

Lying in the low brush were four bodies. They were not wearing German uniforms or even normal clothing. They wore metal armor, like the segments of an armadillo's skin, and red tunics. Their legs were bare and their feet clad in thick sandals. On the heads were metal helmets.

"These guys were shot," one man observed. "They all have swords."

More men clustered around, staring at the strange bodies. Someone muttered, "Romans! They are damned Roman legionaries!"

"More of them up this way!" someone else called. "These men have bows and arrows."

Koll bent to pick up the radio, and his nose wrinkled at the sharp tang of blood. One body was of an archer, a strung bow lying across his mangled chest. At least twenty arrows were stuck into the soil next to him, ready for use. Koll felt like he had entered some strange sort of fantasy world or nightmare. "Keep looking," he said hoarsely.

As they moved up the line of trucks, more dead Romans were found. Dozens, then scores, lying in heaps in the shrubbery and on the roadway. Their dead hands clutched bloody swords and spears. The holes in the armor and bodies left no doubt as to the cause of death. Several of the wooden shields were splintered with holes.

Soon over a hundred Germans and almost as many Romans had been found, and there were still a lot of trucks up the road. There was little reason to wonder what they would hold.

Koll called Weber. "Weber, you have to call someone. We don't know what this is all about. But we are finding the bodies of what I am assured are Roman legionaries. All dead from gunshot wounds. Over."

Weber, usually efficient and prompt, took a long time to respond. "I don't think I copied your last statement, Colonel. Please amplify. Over."

"Oh, you heard me correctly," Koll said, a grim set to his jaw. "Romans. Here are dead men wearing Roman armor. We can see hundreds of them all around." He walked along the line of trucks and bodies. In all his years as a professional soldier, Lieutenant Colonel Eugen Koll had never imagined anything like this. It was like something from a science-fiction film. Gebirgsjäger troops. Men wearing the same uniforms and insignia, carrying the same weapons, and driving in the same trucks. It was as though Gebirgsjäger 232 had been cloned. And murdered. By men from ancient Rome.

Weber's voice cut into his reverie. "Colonel? Are you still there? Over."

"Yes, Weber," Koll said with a voice as dry as sand. "I was distracted. Call someone who can tell us who these men are. Over."

"Who should I call? Over."

How about the Vatican? Koll didn't say. "I don't know. Let someone else figure that out. We're continuing our search. Koll out."

The dumbfounded soldiers continued up the bloody road of dead German troops and Roman legionaries.

Braden, followed by the others, jumped into a Landespolizei van whose engine was already running. Before he could say anything to the driver, Schroeder arrived and pushed his way into the last empty seat. "Get to the west gate now!"

With a squeal of burning rubber, the van turned and drove out of the parking area. It was obvious that Schroeder was agitated. A few tense minutes later, they arrived at a large staging area by the gate where three big military trucks were being loaded with armed Landespolizei troops. Schroeder jumped out and ran to the first truck with a speed that belied his bulk. In moments the trucks were moving with the van following.

Braden held on to the ceiling handle as the van climbed up the slopes to the ridge of the southern Rothaar Mountain range. After the harrowing drive up the winding road, Braden heard the screech of tires ahead. A moment later, their driver hit his brakes and stopped. Braden looked out the front window, but the big trucks blocked his view of the road. To either side were steep rocky escarpments and boulders. They were at the top of the ridge.

"You stay here until we make sure it is safe," their driver said over his shoulder. "The Landespolizei team will secure the area." Then he opened the door and jumped out.

Braden and the others found themselves alone. He was as tight as a drum, and Ann put her cool hand on his. "Be patient, love. They know what they're doing."

He squeezed her hand and tried to smile, but every instinct in his body told him to get out and see what was happening. He could only imagine a scene filled with torn Roman bodies without a single survivor.

He jumped when Captain Rudolf Bach yelled, "Move out and look for survivors!"

That was too much for Braden and he climbed out. The rest were not far behind. Ann carried a police-issue EMT shoulder bag. He ran to the front of the vehicle, but Karl Schroeder stopped him with a raised hand. "Herr Braden, you must stay with the truck. There may still be danger here. We need to assess the situation. Just let my men scout the area. There are several bodies and we need to find out if anyone with weapons is still in the vicinity."

Braden almost pushed his way past the police official but nodded. "Just don't make us wait until it's too late. Please."

Schroeder gave him an understanding smile. "You will be called in as soon as it is safe, Herr Braden." Then he turned and walked away.

Morley and the others came over. "What did he say?" the Englishman asked.

"We have to wait until it's safe," Braden told them.

Morley nodded. "That's fine. I'm not especially trained for this sort of thing."

"I know, but I have to get out there and see what's happened."

After ten interminable minutes, Rabble moved forward, keeping the next truck between him and any potential danger. He came back a minute later.

"See anything?" Braden asked anxiously.

"There are some fallen trees across the road just beyond the ridge-line," Rabble said. "Past that are some trucks and a military staff car. The Landespolizei team is running all over the place."

"Did you see any Romans?" Morley asked.

Rabble shook his head. "The road slopes down from there and the brush is pretty thick." Then he turned. "Hold on, Schroeder's coming back."

Braden saw the portly police official returning. He waved for them to come to him. His normally florid face was ashen.

"Are you okay, Herr Commissioner?" Sharon asked him.

Schroeder didn't answer right away. Then he rubbed his eyes. "I have never seen anything like this in my entire life. It's a damned slaughter-house. Hundreds of dead soldiers." He looked at Morley. "You were right, Professor. The Romans did just what you warned me about."

Braden was stunned. Even though he'd been prepared, it was still a shock. "Hundreds? All dead?"

With a nod, Schroeder said, "So far. An entire battalion of Gebirgs-sjäger troops. Three hundred men, massacred."

Braden swallowed, knowing how thoughtless his next question sounded. "Did you find any survivors among the Romans?"

"No," Schroeder said. He gritted his teeth. "How could this happen? A whole battalion of armed men cut down like animals."

Morley said, "I'm sorry, Herr Commissioner. I know this has to be a terrible thing for you. But we still need to find out more. Can we go and see?"

The German official took a deep breath. "Yes. Follow me." The mere act of walking seemed to be a great effort for him. He led the way past the felled evergreens, and the first thing Braden saw was a BMW staff car with both front doors and right back door open. Lying prone behind the steering wheel was a dead man wearing the uniform of a Bundeswehr sergeant. Protruding from his head was the shaft of an arrow.

In the back seat was another body. His chest bore a gaping wound that had to have carved his heart in two. His blood ran like crimson waterfalls onto the road.

Braden was about to continue, but Schroeder stopped by the front passenger door. He bent closer. There was a sharp intake of breath. "You! How the hell did you come to be here?"

Braden saw Schroeder searching the pockets of another dead German officer. But instead of treating the body with respect, the Landespolizei

Commissioner was shoving him over to get at the back pockets. "You're going to tell me one way or another," he growled. Then he yanked a radio from his belt. "This is Schroeder. I need a secure line to the Koblenz data center at once! Also, set up roadblocks on the A60 at the B45 junction. Then get a full crime scene investigation team to the pass on the A60. Get every available unit you can find." He listened for a moment. "Ehlers. I need you to ID someone at once. Drop what you are doing. I'm going to e-mail you some photos. They won't be good but do what you can." He pulled a cell phone from his jacket and began taking pictures of the dead officer, then moved to the back seat and shot more of the one lying there. A moment later, he was back on the radio. "I just sent them to you. Get on it now, Ehlers!"

Crime scene? Braden didn't see what had triggered this reaction. His eyes went wide as he moved forward into the open. Under and around the army trucks were more bodies wearing the mottled light and dark gray fatigue uniforms of the Gebirgsjäger. They clutched black G36 assault rifles in dead hands. He felt a cold pit in his chest while he watched the Landespolizei team continue to scour the woods and vehicles for bodies and survivors. Then he heard Morley calling his name. "Alex! Over here!"

He jogged over and stopped in his tracks. On the ground before him, lying in small knots in the thick brush, were over a dozen dead Roman legionaries. For long moments he said nothing, totally overwhelmed by the sight. The Romans were real. It wasn't an illusion. Braden felt dizzy, but he realized it was because he was not breathing.

Sharon bent to examine the bodies. She looked at Braden. "They've been dead only a short time, perhaps an hour. The blood hasn't coagulated yet." She waved away the flies already buzzing around the open wounds.

Braden looked all around him. More Romans lay near the trucks. Several had died in poses of action, as if they'd been killed as they ran at the Germans. Not one was lying in peaceful repose. Their hands held blood-streaked swords and spears. "They died hard, but they had no chance against those rifles."

Morley sighed. "It looks like they gave as good as they got, though."

"Yes," Braden said in a hollow voice. Walking among the bodies, he felt something crunch under his shoe. It was an empty 5.56mm cartridge. He picked it up. It was warm from the sun. Around the German bodies were hundreds more, glinting like brass confetti. He surveyed the grisly scene.

Rabble came over. "How do you say 'payback's a bitch' in Latin?"

"Yeah," Braden said slowly, still holding the cartridge. "Lucius finally did what he set out to do."

Rabble turned to look at him. "Oh, he did a lot more than that, Alex."

"What do you mean?" Braden said.

Rabble swept his hand to encompass the macabre scene. "This is not what it appears to be. Something isn't right."

Braden shot him a hard look. "No shit something isn't right, Barn. It's a catastrophe. And the entire world will go apeshit when it gets out."

Rabble didn't respond to Braden's sarcasm. He looked at Schroeder at the BMW. "What's got Schroeder so worked up?"

Braden glanced back. Schroeder was still talking on the radio, gesticulating into thin air. "I don't know," he said. "I think he recognized someone in that staff car."

"Hmm," Rabble murmured. "Interesting." He had that look on his face again.

"Barn, what the hell are you going on about?"

"I think something totally unexpected happened."

Braden could not believe what he was hearing. "What could be more unexpected than a bunch of Romans wiping out a German Army battalion?"

Rabble pointed at the cartridge in Braden's hand. "Where did that come from?"

"Are you blind? There are thousands of the goddamned things. Look!"

"I know that," Rabble persisted. "Look at that cartridge in your hand. What is it?"

"A spent 5.56 millimeter. Standard NATO issue."

"Right," Rabble said with a raised eyebrow. "You remember what Worden told us? The Gebirgsjäger had no live ammo at hand. How in the hell did they manage to put up a fight?"

Braden surveyed the battlefield. Within his sight were at least fifty German soldiers and as many Romans. Every German was holding a rifle and surrounded by spent brass. He had no answer.

"This ambush was very quick," Rabble said. "The Romans shot arrows into the stopped trucks and killed scores of Germans right off." He turned and leaned into the load bed of the nearest truck. A moment later, he emerged, holding something in his hand. "God, it looks like a slaughterhouse in there." He held out an ammunition clip. "Take a look."

Braden looked at the clip. It was full with thirty rounds. "What about it?"

"These are live rounds. I pulled this from the bandolier of one of the dead soldiers. He never even left the truck. That means these men had live ammo from the start."

Braden absently ran his fingers over the round in his hands as he thought about what Rabble was saying. And suddenly he realized his friend was right. "But if they weren't supposed to have ammo, how did they get it?"

"These men were already fully armed," Rabble said.

"What are you getting at, Barn?"

Rabble shook his head. "I'm not absolutely sure yet. But I have a feeling we're going to find out that Lucius did us all a very big favor."

Before Braden could give the matter further thought, Morley called to him. "Alex. We've found an officer."

He and Rabble rushed to the far side of the road. Morley was bent over a Roman. The man was clad in the armor of a Roman officer with a bedraggled crossways crest of horsehair on the helmet. The man was heavily muscled and tall. His eyes were closed, his face rugged, with a stubble of dark beard. Unlike the others, this man had been posed with his hands folded across his chest.

Braden bit his lip. "Which one was he, I wonder?"

Morley bent over and reached into the dead man's haversack. "Ah," he said as his hand withdrew from the dirty leather bag. Then he stood and held out what he'd found.

Braden's eyes widened. "A Walther PP pistol." He took the small handgun from Morley and examined it. After sliding the clip from the magazine, he said, "It's been fired. Only one round left."

Morley nodded. "I think this was taken from St. Paul or Dumont in Belgium."

"Then this man has to be either Lucius, Marcus, or Septimus."

"Probably," Morley replied, still looking at the dead Roman. "We may never know."

Braden pushed the empty clip back into the pistol. "The safety is off and the hammer cocked." He regarded the dead officer. "It's a wonder he didn't blow his foot off."

Suddenly they heard voices from down the road. They all turned to see more soldiers approaching, dressed in combat fatigues and armed with rifles. For just an instant, Braden thought he would be witness to another massacre, but one of the Landespolizei team held up his shotgun. "Halt! Identify yourselves at once!"

An officer at the head of the group stopped and held his pistol up and away from his body. "Lieutenant Colonel Eugen Koll, Gebirgsjäger Battalion 232. We are stopped down the road. Who are you?"

The policeman lowered his weapon but remained wary. "Landespolizei Response Team. I am Sergeant Maybach. We have been looking for survivors from your unit."

The man named Koll shook his head. "Not our unit." He waved his hand around the bloody scene. "These men are impostors."

Then Karl Schroeder arrived, out of breath. He faced the colonel. "I am Commissioner Karl Schroeder, Landespolizei. Can you prove your identity?"

The military officer frowned as if this were an unreasonable request but reached into his pocket. Sliding out a thin wallet, he opened it to show the card to Schroeder.

Schroeder examined the card and handed it back. "Thank you, Colonel Koll." He held out his hand and the colonel shook it.

"Do you have any idea what happened here?" Koll asked.

"I was hoping you could tell me," Schroeder said with a faint smile. "What was that you said? These men are impostors?"

Koll gave him an emphatic nod. "That's right. Not a single one has identification, yet all are supposedly from this unit. All of my men are accounted for."

"All of them?" Schroeder's body tensed.

"Yes," Koll said, indicating the men behind him. "Two companies are with me, and the other one is waiting down the road past the other felled trees."

Schroeder almost seemed to smile, then asked, "Have you found any survivors?"

Koll nodded. "Two wounded men, but both are deep in shock. My medics are tending to them."

He turned when Altmeyer came over. "Yes, Lieutenant?"

"Colonel," the younger officer began, "we found four more survivors. But they are not wounded. They were hiding under two of the trucks among the dead. They refused to identify themselves. We disarmed and searched them. No identification. Sergeant Wulff has them under guard."

This time Schroeder did smile. "Good. We are going to talk to them." He opened his mouth to say something else when a shout came from down the road.

"Uncle Karl!"

Schroeder turned to see a soldier running toward him. "Helmut? Is that you?"

"Yes, Uncle Karl!" The soldier came up and stopped, saluting his commanding officer. He seemed embarrassed. "My apologies, Colonel. This is my uncle."

Koll nodded. "Ah. I see. Very well, carry on." He saluted the elder Schroeder. "We will talk more later, Herr Commissioner." Then he turned away, walking back down the road.

"Helmut," Schroeder said, holding his nephew's hand, "I feared you were dead." He was smiling despite the carnage around them. "We thought this was your unit."

The young man shook his head and slung the safed G36 over his shoulder. "No, it's not. A group of perfect fakes, but not us."

"I am glad," Schroeder said with a grin. "I would be terrified to tell Else and Kurt of the death of their only son."

Helmut grinned. "I wouldn't be too thrilled about it either, Uncle Karl. Mama's reaction would make being dead a blessing."

Then the soldier paused, looking at the bodies, the blood, the Romans, and modern and ancient weapons. "Uncle Karl, what happened here? Who are these men, the ones dressed like Roman legionaries?"

Only two days before, Karl Schroeder would have said they were madmen, fanatics and lunatics. But now, viewing the worst scene he'd ever witnessed in his decades as a cop, he simply said, "They are real Roman legionaries. They had a mission of revenge to accomplish. And I think they did just that."

His nephew merely raised an eyebrow, and the uncle studied him. Perhaps his young relative was more easily able to accept the unacceptable than he.

Schroeder rubbed his chin. "And the others, I don't know yet. But I intend to find out." He exhaled. "I have work to do. Please come find me at the rally later if there is time." He hugged the boy—man, he realized. A soldier.

Helmut saluted by touching the edelweiss emblem on his dark green beret and turned back to find his sergeant.

To Braden, Karl Schroeder looked like a condemned man who had just received a reprieve. He picked up his radio. "Ehlers, this is Schroeder. What do you have for me? Over." He listened for some minutes, then replied, "Very good. I'll be back soon. Keep looking. Out."

"The Romans' bodies are deteriorating," Sharon Kelly said with alarm and bewilderment. "I don't understand. If they lived this long, the plant residue is still in their cells and tissues. Just being killed should not purge it in just a short time." She was almost frantic. "I have to get some tissue samples," she said, searching her small carry bag for something to use. "If I can get some analysis, I might be able to find some way of preserving them longer."

Ann rummaged through her EMT bag. "I think I have what you need, Sharon." She pulled out a small plastic case and opened it. "Here, this might work. An emergency field surgery kit." She withdrew a scalpel, scissors, and some small glassine bags. "Let me help you."

"I'll take all the help I can get," Sharon said as the two women bent to their task. She used the scissors to snip bits of flesh from the Romans' necks, hair, and the insides of their mouths.

Sharon worked frantically, racing against time. In a way, Braden realized, she was two thousand years too late.

"Barney," Sharon said without turning her head. "I need dry ice. As much as you can get, and body bags or human remains transport containers. ASAP!"

Rabble was on his phone at once. "On it."

Morley used Sharon's phone to take scores of photos of the Roman bodies, weapons, and even the wounds. It was a simple task yet had never been done in the history of the world. Professor Arthur Morley was calmly taking photographs of citizens of Ancient Rome.

Rabble said, "A helicopter is bringing as much dry ice here as can be found right away. And they're sending a complete field forensics team as well. We'll get everything you need."

Braden had been silent throughout this. Then he spoke. "I wonder where the rest of them are."

Rabble and Morley turned to look at him. He was staring into the woods, his brow furrowed. "They can't all be dead," he said. "I don't believe they are." He looked to where Schroeder and Koll were talking. "I'll be right back."

Braden introduced himself to Koll and produced his NATO credentials. "I would like to speak with your prisoners, Colonel Koll."

The colonel frowned, but Schroeder said, "Please let him pass. I want to see what they say to him before I try to interrogate them."

Koll relented and asked Braden to follow him. "You may not have much luck," he said. "None of them have said a word since we found them."

"I have nothing to lose by trying." The officer led Braden to one of the trucks. Three armed soldiers stood guard around four men sitting on the ground. Their hands were bound with zip ties. They all wore the uniforms of the Gebirgsjäger with the edelweiss patch. One man had a bandage around his head, but otherwise, they appeared uninjured.

Koll nodded to the sergeant in charge of the guard detail. "This is Herr Braden of NATO. He wishes to speak with these men."

Sergeant Wulff stepped back, but he and his men kept their rifles at the ready.

Braden stood in front of the oldest man, who wore a sergeant's insignia. "My name is Alex Braden," he said in German. "I am an investigator with NATO. Can you tell me who you are?" He saw Schroeder standing nearby, out of sight of the prisoners.

The men remained silent, their dirty, blood-spattered faces bearing identical expressions of shock and defiance. A strange mixture, given the circumstances. "Can you tell me what happened here?"

Still there was no response. "We know you are not genuine Gebirgsjäger troops. Whatever your mission was, it is no longer an issue. All I want is for you to tell me what happened here."

The bogus sergeant sneered at Braden. "You have no authority here, Amerikaner," he said, a look of sheer hatred in his eyes.

Braden was about to reply when Schroeder came over. "This man is here on my authority and that of the German Government. You will answer his questions." Schroeder's face was a mask of pure loathing and rage as he leaned close. "It is only a matter of time."

The man shrank back. "We have no intention of saying anything to you."

Schroeder cocked an eyebrow. "I suspect Herr Horst Molders might be more forthcoming."

"Molders? He is alive?" The man's face went white.

"Yes," Schroeder said with a smirk. "He is being taken to a hospital right now under heavy sedation. I don't think I need to tell you what a suspected enemy of the state can be induced to say when under such drugs."

Braden thought Schroeder sounded just like one of the evil Nazi interrogators in an old war movie.

The four men exchanged horrified looks. Braden didn't know what Schroeder was up to but remained silent.

The police official glared at them. "He did mumble a few things before he was taken away. Josef Hauser and your NOD are dead, but soon we will know everything."

Braden was totally dumbfounded. What was Schroeder talking about?

Schroeder leaned close. "If you refuse to cooperate, it will be very bad for you. I need not tell you what the current federal penalty is for domestic terrorism."

Braden suddenly remembered what Rabble had said about Lucius doing them a big favor. These men were terrorists.

"I will not make this offer again." Schroeder turned his back on the impostors and strode off.

For several seconds no one said anything. Then Braden cleared his throat. "Look, all I want to know is what happened here today. I don't care about your mission."

The four men seemed to wilt as they surveyed the dead men around them. Then, without meeting Braden's eyes, the bogus sergeant said, "We were moving up the road and were stopped by the fallen trees." His voice was tinged with nervousness. "Before the trucks even stopped, arrows started coming through the canvas sides. Our men were killed without any warning."

Rabble arrived and listened. He had a curious smirk on his face as the man continued.

"The drivers and all who were in the open were killed right away. It was cold-blooded murder."

Another prisoner spoke up. "Some of us got out and tried to return fire. But we could not find cover. It was a massacre. They murdered our men without mercy. Even when we shot them down, more swarmed out of the woods and attacked."

"Yes," said the first man. "I was once a prison guard. I saw a riot years ago, very bloody and savage. But nothing like this. These devils killed as if they enjoyed it."

I'm sure they did, Braden thought. "What happened next?"

A third man spoke, obviously wanting to appear cooperative. "The enemy were on both sides of the road and shooting from the brush. We tried to find them to shoot, but each time we exposed ourselves, a storm of arrows and spears came at us. They ran at us and we shot many, but there were always more. They never stopped coming." He shook his head at the memory. "Savages. They butchered every man they found."

"How did you survive?" Braden asked.

The first man said, "I was under one truck and every man by me was dead. I suppose they did not see me."

The others nodded as if to say they had escaped being slaughtered the same way.

Braden glanced at the bodies heaped under the trucks. "And then what?"

"They stopped," said the second man. "Just like that, they stopped the killing. Some were coming right at us with their swords, but a yell from a man, I think was an officer, stopped them. And then they just backed away."

"How many did you see still living? You obviously killed hundreds.

"Not as many as I wish I had," the first man said between clenched teeth. "I think twenty or thirty."

"You saw them leave?"

"I did, because I hated them so much I wanted to find a way to kill all the rest. They destroyed our dream."

"And what dream is that," Sergeant Wulff asked. He didn't bother to conceal his anger at the men who sullied the proud edelweiss emblem. His knuckles turned white on the stock of his assault rifle.

The impostor swallowed and looked at Braden. "Do you have any other questions, Amerikaner?"

"Just one," Braden said. "Which way did they leave?"

The man said nothing for several seconds. Then he pointed with his chin. "That way. North."

CHAPTER V

HEROES OF THE FATHERLAND

As the legionaries walked north, the forest covered the straggling line of men in a protective embrace. They were the last, the very last Roman legionaries in the world. Lucius led the small group with the centuria Remus Draconius at his side. He thought not about the last few days and the fortune the gods had given them but the days to come.

He wanted to finish the long journey that began in Rome countless ages before. There was no reason to return to Rome, if it even existed anymore. And even if it did, he doubted the modern citizens would welcome the last survivors of Legio LIV as conquering heroes on the street of triumph with rose petals strewn in their path.

The world had once been a quiet land of green hills and tilled soil, where life moved at the slow pace of the horse. Long gone was the sweet taste of wine and clean-smelling air. The sounds of the wind, the twitter of birds, and the burble of running water in a stream were all familiar in his memory. But now, the world had become bewilderingly fast, loud, smelly, frenetic, huge, and unknowable. It was not their world, their life. That had passed uncounted centuries ago. All they had known and understood and loved was long gone in the dust of the ages.

Lucius did not have to poll his surviving legionaries. He could see it in their eyes, their movements, and their countenance. They were nearly finished, only duty and honor placing one foot before the other. They doggedly marched on, focused only on their distant goal. It was time for them all to rest. Forever.

He and his devoted soldiers had earned it. So many had died in the dark of the cellar, on the long march, and in battle, but all had earned their place among the stars. Septimus, Marcus, Vitellus, Plutonius, and all the others awaited the last remaining legionaries.

Soon, Lucius would lay down on soil consecrated in the blood of heroes and martyrs. He loved every one of these men. The hatred and bloodlust for vengeance had passed. Their duty done, he no longer felt anger. Now, all Lucius Cassius Aquilius wanted was peace. It lay ahead in the forests of Germania. And if the gods were generous, he would see his wife and son again.

He smiled at the thought. *Soon. Very soon.*

Ambulances and paramedic trucks arrived on scene from both east and west, disgorging dozens of EMTs and doctors. Braden watched as Sharon supervised placing the body of the Roman officer into a body bag, then into a large plastic case packed with dry ice. Billows of white smoke foamed over the edges as they worked.

Schroeder came over. "What did you learn from the prisoners?" he asked Braden as they watched the Romans being carried away.

"There are at least thirty Romans still alive," Braden said.

Schroeder turned to look at him. "Where did they go? To Rome?"

Braden had to smile. "I'm surprised at you, Herr Commissioner. A few days ago, you as much as called me a lunatic. Now you seem to believe in the Romans."

The older man gave him a weak grin. "I suppose it might have been prudent to listen to reason."

Braden laughed. "Reason? I don't recall reason ever entering this bizarre situation."

Morley and Rabble joined them.

"We're trying to determine where Lucius may be right now," Braden said. "What do you think, Arthur? Would they go to Rome?"

The Englishman rubbed his jaw for a moment. "I don't believe they're going to Rome. They must understand the Rome they knew is long gone. There's nothing for them there. It was all about their revenge and honor. They lost friends and comrades, even family, in the Varian massacre. It's time for them to rejoin their fallen comrades."

"Yes," Braden said with a nod. "That's what I thought, too."

Schroeder looked confused. "'Rejoin their fallen comrades?' Who? The ones back in the cellar in France?"

"No," Morley replied. "In the Teutoburg Forest at a hill called Kalkriese. Where Varus and his three legions were ambushed and slaughtered two thousand years ago."

The police official fixed Morley with a long stare. "You're sure?"

"As sure as I can be," Morley said with a shrug.

"The job they set out to do is done," said Braden. "Their honor is avenged, and now it's time to rest."

Schroeder looked northward. "The Teutoburger Wald would be many days' march from here. Can they reach it?"

"I don't know," Braden admitted. "But after what I've seen today, I would be the last person in the world to bet against them."

"Do you feel we should let them go?" Schroeder asked him.

Braden was surprised. "Are you serious?"

Schroeder remained silent. His face was unreadable.

Braden glanced at Morley. "Well, I don't think we can just let them go. But I have to admit, I'm rooting for them."

"'Rooting for them?'" Schroeder said, perplexed.

"Cheering them on," Braden said.

"Ah, I see. I can understand that, but the fact remains that these Romans have murdered German citizens, stolen livestock, and, if you wish to split hairs, entered the country illegally."

"And let's not forget what they did here," Braden said, wondering why that hadn't been the first thing on Schroeder's list of crimes.

"Yes. That too." There was a smug expression on Schroeder's face. "They did indeed." He paused, for effect, as it turned out. "Thank God for that."

Both Morley and Braden exchanged puzzled looks. "What?" Braden asked. He caught another knowing look on Rabble's face. "What's going on here?"

Schroeder appeared happy to have the upper hand for a change. "Our Roman friends did the people of Germany a great service. This column was composed of members of a group known as the New Order of Deutschland, or NOD. They are a large radical nationalist terrorist organization that has instigated riots and acts of violence in Germany over the last year."

Braden stared at Schroeder in astonishment. "You knew about this?"

"No, not until a short time ago," Schroeder admitted. "I recognized one of the men in that staff car. His name was Horst Molders, a former Bundeswehr officer who had been involved in violent anti-NATO demonstrations some years ago. Molders was implicated in two bombings, but we could never get an indictment. But his name and face were on the watch list. When I saw him in the car, I called Koblenz and put them to work on it."

"What have you found out?" Rabble asked.

Schroeder said, "We're still looking, but it appears these men intended to take the place of the genuine Bundeswehr unit and act as the Chancellor's honor guard. I found their plans in the staff car. But they, unlike the authentic unit, were armed. They intended to hold hostage and, if necessary, kill Chancellor Hoffman, his party, and innocent civilians."

"For what purpose?" Morley asked, his eyes wide.

"To bring about the birth of a new Germany," Schroeder explained. "A pure, racially isolated Germany. One with no foreign blood, business, or military presence. A man named Josef Hauser was in the back seat of the staff car. He was the leader of the NOD. His father was accidentally killed by an American tank when he was a boy, and since then, he has been active with several ultra-conservative nationalist German groups."

"Wow," Braden said as he looked around him. "What a catastrophe that would have been."

Schroeder sighed. "We had absolutely no idea this was coming. We never heard a thing about any plans to attack the rally. It was only your Romans who foiled Hauser's plans."

Braden realized how much that had cost Schroeder to admit. "Is this NOD, or whatever you called it, out of business now?"

"Not yet," Schroeder said, shaking his head. "This is only the action element. Others are awaiting their cue to move. But we are taking steps to find and round them up. Our biggest task is to keep them from learning of this. If the rest of the NOD find out, they'll scatter." He looked toward the Bundeswehr officers. "I urged Colonel Koll and his officers to refrain from saying anything about this matter on the radio. Right now, I am instituting a total news and radio blackout. No one outside this area can learn of the attack on the NOD."

"Who else is involved?" Rabble asked.

"It's too early to say, but I suspect it goes into the highest levels of the German government."

Koll stood close by with one of his officers, listening to the conversation. Braden realized how lucky the entire battalion was to be alive. "If the real battalion had arrived just a few minutes earlier . . ." He left the rest unsaid.

"Yes," Schroeder said. "It was so close."

Braden looked at the dead around them. "As sure as I was, I never really imagined they could do something like this."

"Thank God they did," Schroeder said. "Otherwise, right now, we'd be frantically trying to save a lot of innocent lives and bargain with a large group of armed terrorists holding the Chancellor hostage." Then, inexplicably, the police official began to laugh. His face turned red, and his belly shook with mirth. The others watched him in astonishment. At last, Schroeder pulled a handkerchief from his pocket and wiped his eyes. "I'm sorry. I know this is serious, but I was just thinking that I should arrange for your Roman friends to receive medals for services to the state."

For a long moment, there was only the sound of the EMTs and Landespolizei teams in the background. Then Morley started to laugh. "Oh, I wish I could be there when you inform Lucius that he and his men are Heroes of the Fatherland!" For a full minute, the four men laughed. Braden saw some of the Landespolizei team staring at them with frank curiosity.

Predictably, Rabble was the first to regain his composure. "We need to find them, and fast."

"I know," Braden said, "but how do we do that? They proved to be impossible to find when there were hundreds of them. Now there may be less than fifty."

"Can we borrow some assets from the military?" Rabble inquired.

A canny look crossed Schroeder's face. "Let's call General Worden." The police official reached to his belt and pulled off the radio. Braden was about to take it when Schroeder said, "Ah, sorry. Wrong one. Here." He handed another one over after switching it on.

Braden took it, seeing that it was a sophisticated Siemens satellite radio. Just as he was about to raise it to his mouth, he felt something sticky on the keypad. It looked like spatters of dried blood. He keyed the "Transmit" button. "General Worden, this is Alex Braden. Over." He heard a bark of static, and then Worden's deep voice came from the speaker. "Oh, ah . . . Herr Braden. How did you get on this frequency?"

At that moment, a look of triumph crossed Schroeder's face. "Do not tell him I gave it to you."

With a perplexed nod, Braden keyed the button. "I don't know, General. I'm using a radio provided by . . . er, the Landespolizei."

"Very well," Worden said, still sounding confused. "What is your situation? Over."

"General, we need your help again. Can you requisition a helicopter? We need to conduct a search in the woods. I believe you know what we're looking for." He was careful not to mention the Romans over the airwaves. He noticed that both Schroeder and Rabble were watching him with keen interest.

The general's response was slow. "I understand you need to do this, Herr Braden, but we are on a high alert right now. We may not be able to release those assets just yet. What is the current situation up there? Over."

Schroeder put his hand on Braden's arm. "We don't want to put out any information on the airwaves. Please don't say anything about what happened here. Tell him we have it all under control, and there is no more threat to the rally."

With a nod, Braden keyed the button again. "General, all is under control. There is no further threat at this time. But we really need a helicopter. It's urgent."

Schroeder nodded, smiling.

For a long moment, Worden said nothing, then told Braden to hold. He came back on. "We are sending you two helicopters from the search teams at once. They can be there in two hours. You may use them at your discretion. Over."

"Thank you, General," Braden said. "I'll keep you informed. Out."

He handed the radio back to Schroeder, who accepted it with a smile and turned it off. "It seems General Worden will assist in your search. Again."

"I want to find them before anyone else does," Braden said.

"Who else would be looking for them?" Schroeder said.

"The press, of course," Braden replied without emotion. "That would be a disaster."

Rabble nodded. "As bad as it has been, that would be ten times worse. The media down at the rally must have noted the EMTs and ambulances leaving. They'll be on the scent by now."

"Can we keep them from finding out about this?" Morley asked. He looked up at the cloudless sky. "They have helicopters. They could see and film everything from up there."

"No worries about that, Professor," Rabble said calmly. "The German Luftwaffe and Air Traffic Control declared an air exclusion zone within fifty kilometers of the rally. That covers this too. No civilian aircraft can approach the area."

"That's good to hear," Morley said. "But don't forget those annoying drone things. Anyone can purchase the bloody things."

Rabble glanced at Schroeder. "I remember something about an anti-drone jamming system used around your military bases. Can one of those be brought here and set up?"

Schroeder nodded. "There is one at the rally. It also covers a radius of fifty kilometers. The rally organizers were adamant about not allowing unauthorized aircraft or UAVs to penetrate the exclusion zone. Any drone coming close will fall out of the sky."

"There you go, Professor," Rabble said with a confident smile. "But it's only a matter of time before the media find out about this. We have to move fast."

After Schroeder left to deal with the prisoners, Braden put his hand on Rabble's arm. "You sneaky son of a bitch. You knew about this, didn't you?"

"Well, not exactly," his friend said with an amused look. "I just had a feeling not everything was kosher here."

"A feeling?" Braden asked him in confusion. "That's all?"

Rabble shrugged. "Sometimes, when you're building a jigsaw puzzle, you find a piece that simply doesn't belong. And that's the one I focus on. When I saw those thousands of empty cartridges, it triggered my instincts."

"You might have told me sooner, Barn," Braden said with an exasperated shake of his head.

Rabble laughed. "And spoil Schroeder's moment of triumph? You saw the look on his face. He'll come out of this looking good, take my word for it."

"How can you say that? He almost blew it. It was only the Romans' attack on this NOD group that saved his ass."

"Al," Rabble said, still grinning, "Karl Schroeder might be a narrow-minded pugnacious bureaucratic asshole, but he is one hell of a good cop. He's got something going on that we don't know about."

"Any ideas?" Braden prompted him.

"A few," Rabble said. "I'm thinking about that radio."

"The one he handed to me? It had blood on the keypad. Did you notice?"

Rabble looked at the scene around them. "Lots of that around here."

Seeing he wasn't going to get anything more from his friend, Braden let the matter drop.

Koll and Bentele led the Gebirgsjäger troops back to where the other two companies waited.

Bentele said, "I'm concerned about this news blackout regarding our status. We cannot contact our division headquarters or the Defense

Ministry." He shook his head. "My wife and children, all our families will think us dead."

Koll stopped and faced the major. "I agree, Major, but the Landespolizei commissioner said it's necessary to keep a tight lid on this matter. We do not dare make any radio calls that might get back to these NOD terrorists."

"But for how long?" Bentele asked.

"The commissioner assured me it would be no more than twenty-four hours," Koll said. "For now, we must keep word of our continued survival from leaking. Tell the platoon leaders to order the men not to mention the matter to anyone on their cell phones. In fact, they are not to use their phones for any reason until the blackout is lifted."

Bentele stared at him. "Are you sure, Colonel? The men will be upset about that."

"It is an order," Koll said in a firm but understanding voice. "They're soldiers. We are, in a sense, at war. I do not like it any more than you, but we have no choice. This NOD bund must be found and arrested before they learn of the battle."

Bentele nodded. "I will see that it's done."

"Good," Koll said. "We will learn the truth in time."

Soldiers had pulled the trucks to the shoulders. Sergeant Dorfman leaned on the staff car's fender. Koll went to him and put his hand on the sergeant's shoulder. "Dorfman. If you ever—*ever*—take a wrong turn again, you know what I'm going to do?"

Dorfman, totally at a loss for words, simply shook his head.

"I'll give you a medal," Koll grinned. "You saved all our lives."

CHAPTER VI

HOUNDS AND JACKALS

Braden's worst fears were soon realized. Every major international news service, from CNN to Reuters, had sent teams to cover Hoffman's rally. For the most part, it had been pure vanilla, politicians and speeches. But then, word trickled in that automatic weapons fire was heard in the mountains, and the press, like feral dogs, alert for the scent of blood, began asking questions. Colonel Ortmann told them she would share any information as soon as there were developments. She had been on the radio with Schroeder and told exactly what to say and do.

But then the Landespolizei response team tore out the west gate and headed to the mountains. That sparked the media feeding frenzy.

But Ortmann, suddenly in the spotlight, refused to provide clear answers to the shouted questions. One reporter from ENN tried to get a helicopter to fly him and his camera crew to the site of the battle, but Ortmann stonewalled him. "There is an air exclusion zone covering this rally for a fifty-kilometer radius," she said firmly. "No civilian aircraft are permitted in the area."

But she would soon find that the power of the press could circumvent even this. Several direct calls from the president of an influential German news service convinced the Defense Ministry to allow a single helicopter to fly over the area. Ortmann received the call from the Defense Minister himself. She had no choice. Then she tried to reach Schroeder, but he didn't answer. Having no choice, she informed the reporters that they would be allowed to send a single helicopter to the site.

"You must obey the air traffic control orders," she said, still fuming. "Only four of you can go along, and you are to share your video feed with the other news services." She had at least been able to limit the incursion to that. The news services protested at the loss of exclusivity, but she prevailed. "Those are the rules. One helicopter, four members of the press. This is for your safety as well as that of the public." Her businesslike tone brooked no argument.

An hour after the first sound of gunfire, an Airbus EC120 helicopter took off from the Wetzlar airport carrying four reporters with direct satellite links and cameras.

Braden, Rabble, and Morley helped Sharon lift Roman corpses into body bags filled with dry ice when they heard the sound of a helicopter approaching. After checking his watch, Braden realized it was too early for the German choppers to have arrived from their base near Koblenz.

Suddenly it was upon them, a loud and hostile presence in the sky, hovering only fifty meters over the trees. Rabble swore under his breath as he pointed at the cameras aimed at the scene of death and chaos below. "So much for the exclusion zone," he muttered.

"Now we're sunk," Braden said over the blat of the rotors. "They'll show the whole world."

Morley, trying to keep his hat on, leaned close to him. "They can't hear us, can they?"

Braden shook his head. "No, but they can see everything, and that's too much."

The helicopter continued to hover and move along the road, the cameras and eyes aboard seeing every detail. Braden even saw one camera aimed right at his face, and he glared at it. "Go away," he hissed at the intruder.

Rabble came over, holding his phone. "It's out. The news is already broadcasting the pictures of the massacre, and I've heard them mention the Romans. The government spokesperson is keeping quiet, but it's only a matter of time before somebody leaks the truth."

"Goddamn it," Braden growled. "Where's a missile launcher when you really need one?"

Just then, a van came up the road from the east. It was stopped at the fallen trees by Landespolizei officers, but it disgorged more reporters and cameras.

"The feeding frenzy has begun, Alex," Morley said.

"Yeah," Braden said. "The Romans are the ones I'm afraid will be devoured. They'll never understand and might become violent."

"We have to get to them first," Morley said with a note of panic in his voice.

"Tell me about it. But how do we do that? The choppers Worden promised us are at least an hour away. And even if they do come, the reporters will follow our every move."

Inexplicably a smile broke over the old professor's face. "We need to give the jackals something else to chase. Let's go talk to our friends from the media." With a baffled Braden following him, Morley approached a handsome man in his thirties with carefully combed sandy brown hair. Braden thought he looked familiar.

Morley reached over the tree trunks with his right hand. "Mister Cannell, so good to see you again."

The other man shook it. "Oh, Professor Morley. Good to see you. You're a long way from your cellar."

Morley laughed. "You might say that, Mister Cannell. A great deal has happened since that night."

Braden suddenly realized where he'd seen the younger man before. On ENN, interviewing Morley at the site of the cellar. Another news team moved closer, and he saw the Reuters News Service emblem on the microphone holder's shirt.

Cannell entreated Morley to let him and his crew come around the tree barrier, but the old professor shook his head. "I can't authorize that, but you can talk to the officer in charge, Landespolizei Commissioner Schroeder, if you like."

"That would be great," Cannell said with an expression of triumph on his face. "Where can we find him?" He tried to look past Morley.

"I'll bring him to you." Schroeder was nearby, talking with another officer. Morley went over and had a hurried discussion with the commissioner, none of which Braden could hear. Then both men came over, and Morley introduced Schroeder to Cannell.

Schroeder was clearly not happy to be talking to reporters and said, "I have very little to say at this time."

Cannell didn't waver. He had his microphone out and the cameras running. "Can you at least tell us who was involved? We're hearing about Bundeswehr troops fighting a battle up here."

"We are still investigating," Schroeder said flatly, "and will have a statement later in the day."

"Chancellor Hoffman's honor guard of Gebirgsjäger troops has not arrived at the rally, and we have heard reports that they may have been ambushed. That's over three hundred men. Can you confirm this?"

Schroeder shook his head. "We have no count at this time. We are still attempting to ascertain what happened here and look for survivors."

Then Cannell put a hand to his ear, listening to something on a tiny receiver. A smile broke over his face. "I've just heard from the helicopter camera crew that they've gotten some images of bodies of men wearing Roman legionary armor. Can you verify this?" Then he glanced at Morley, and a shrewd look came over his face. "Professor, is that why you're here? Is there a connection between these men wearing Roman gear and the cellar uncovered in France two weeks ago?"

That's a pretty astute guess, Braden thought, watching Morley, who didn't seem to be in the least bit flustered by the question.

"It's too early to say at this time, and our part in the matter is merely to assist the Landespolizei in their own investigation."

"Did the men dressed as Romans take the armor from the cellar in France?" Cannell asked, still holding the microphone pointed at Morley.

Morley showed a hint of irritation. "Whether the men who did this are connected with the French cellar or not, we will find them and learn the truth."

Braden managed not to groan. Morley had just told the reporter that there were Roman survivors.

The reporter instantly leaned closer to Morley. "Are there survivors? Where are they now?"

Morley and Schroeder exchanged nervous glances. To Braden, it looked almost theatrical.

Cannell smelled blood. "Professor Morley, I asked you, are there survivors? Where are they now?"

Suddenly showing alarm, Morley said, "I didn't say that, Mister Cannell."

Cannell said, "How can a Roman archaeologist help the German police investigate a mass murder?"

The old academician pursed his lips and blurted out, "We're just trying to find them. It's a long journey and lots of open country. They won't be able to hide and we'll find them."

Then Schroeder put his beefy hand on Morley's arm. "I think that's all we have to say at this time." He led Morley away, walking along the fallen trees. Cannell called out, "Professor! Are they going back? To France?" He was now walking along the tree trunks, attempting to keep pace with the agitated archaeologist.

Morley stopped and glared at the reporter. "No, of course not! They won't go west to France."

"Then where are they going? Italy?"

"I don't have anything more to say. We'll find them down there somewhere. Good day." He turned on his heel and strode off, his face a stone mask.

With a smile of triumph, Cannell turned to the camera. "We have an unconfirmed report that a group of armed men wearing Roman legionary uniforms has attacked a German Army unit. The present whereabouts of these men is unknown, but it appears they may be marching south. An extensive search effort by government forces is underway. We'll stay here for the moment but will be back with further developments. This is Jason Cannell, ENN, in the Rothaar Mountains west of Wetzlar, Germany."

Braden glared at the reporter and followed Morley. Rabble was right behind him.

Rabble said, "I think something important just happened and I missed it."

"Really?" Braden said with mock surprise. "That's a first."

Morley was talking with Schroeder when they came up. "Ah, Alex. I think that may have bought us some time."

"How can you say that? You just told the whole world we're looking for Roman survivors loose in Germany."

The old man seemed amused. His anger had disappeared. "I think not. I told him we were looking for survivors. I never said who they were or where they were going."

Just then, the helicopter, which had been flying up and down the road for the last half hour, banked and disappeared to the east. The blat of its rotors diminished, then faded into silence.

"Yes, you did. You said—" Braden stopped, thinking. Then his eyes narrowed. "You let them think the Romans were going south. To Italy."

The Englishman smiled. "I may have intimated that, now you come to mention it. I've been dealing with the press for years. I know how to handle them." Then he clapped a hand on Schroeder's shoulder. "And let's not forget our good friend's stellar performance as an uncooperative police bureaucrat. With him along, I had no trouble manipulating Mister Cannell." He gave Braden a level look. "Alex, I bought us some time, maybe a few hours. It's the best we have. We can use that to our advantage. Let them scurry all over the south looking for them."

Rabble held up his phone. "I'll keep listening to the reports."

Back at the guarded tree barrier, Jason Cannell hit "End Call" on his phone. "That's done." He turned to his videographer. "No way in hell are we staying here while the search is going on. We'll find those Roman guys ourselves. I just called the head office, and they'll get us on that chopper." He jogged over to the Reuters team. He said to the reporter, "Ian, can you stay here and watch for anything on this end? I'll cut you in on what we film."

Ian Tanner, a tall and stoutly built Londoner, said, "I'd bloody well rather be on the helo, but we'll stay on here just in case they open the barrier."

Cannell clapped him on the arm. "You're a good sport, Ian. I'll be back to you as soon as I get on the chopper." With his videographer following, he dashed back down the road to the van.

Braden heard the sound of another approaching helicopter. His watch told him it was half past three in the afternoon. He covered his eyes from the sun and saw two dark insect-like shapes emerging from the clear blue sky in the west. "Blackhawks," he said to himself. "Finally."

Waving to Rabble and Morley, he jogged down the road to a clear grassy field just past a grove of trees. Fortunately, it was out of sight of the remaining cameras at the tree barrier. It was just large enough to allow both military helicopters to land.

After touching down, the beat of the rotors slowed. In a minute, the right-side hatch opened, and the pilot jumped to the ground. Wearing a dark-gray flight suit and helmet with a stylized hawk emblem, the figure waved to the other craft and moved to where Braden waited.

"Herr Braden. I'm Captain Else Klein, 109 Squadron." The pilot pulled off the helmet and held out her hand. Her English was excellent.

Braden took her hand with a smile. "I remember. You're the one whose crew found that nudist camp, right?"

Klein chuckled, shaking her head. "Yes. Even if I make general's rank, the only thing anyone will remember about me is that damned nudist camp."

"That's the way fame is, Captain. But you can do a great service to your country today, if you're willing."

"Of course. I was told to put my ships and crews at your disposal." She turned her head to see three more men in flight suits coming over. "Ah, there we are."

The others, all men, took off their helmets as Klein introduced them. "My co-pilot, Lieutenant Werner Roebach."

The young man shook Braden's hand. Then Klein gestured to the other men. "From number Niner-Three is Lieutenant Siegfried Haase and Flight Sergeant Walter Szell."

Rabble and Morley had arrived and introduced themselves.

"I understand we are again looking for Romans," Klein said, getting the meeting on track.

"Yes," said Braden. "I know this is hard to believe, but—"

He was cut off by Klein's upraised hand. "I don't find it hard to believe. That arrow hit my ship. I know there are Romans out there. And as we came in for landing," she said, surveying the distant road littered with bodies and stopped trucks, "we could see hundreds of Roman bodies. I presume we are looking for survivors?"

"We are," Braden said, glad he didn't have to convince the aviators. "We believe them to be headed north and are probably within ten kilometers, perhaps fifteen."

"In the woods?" Roebach asked, looking to the north.

"Probably. They want to remain hidden. They normally marched at night, but in this case, I think they're trying to put as much distance between themselves and this place as possible."

Klein checked her watch. "There are about five hours of daylight left, but as you know, we can search at night." She ran a hand through her short, sweaty hair. "How many are we looking for?"

"At least twenty, but no more than forty. We have to find them before the press does."

Klein snorted. "The press are also hunting them?"

Braden nodded. "We need to keep them at a distance and not lead them right to the Romans. Can we decoy them somehow?"

Klein smiled wickedly at Braden. "I will be happy to do that. Let's come up with a plan, shall we?"

The arrival of the two helicopters did not go unnoticed by the reporters at the tree barrier. They watched and waited, but nothing new happened for another fifteen minutes. Then, the whine of turbine engines and rotors filled the air as the Nachtfalkes lifted off again.

Ian Tanner was on his cell phone. "Jason, this is Tanner. We're still here. The two German Army Blackhawks just took off. They're headed out now, both going south in a bloody big hurry." He had to cover his other ear to hear over the noise. "No. That fat Hun cop still refuses to let us in. Okay, we'll stay here. But don't forget about us." He clicked off and told his videographer, "Cannell is in the chartered chopper. They're going to stick to those Hun choppers like glue. When they find the blokes who killed all those troopers, we'll be let into the video feed."

The videographer's face showed skepticism. "I wouldn't bet on it, Ian. Cannell's not one to share the glory."

"Don't I know it," Tanner said, looking back toward the south. "That bastard stiffed me for that story on that Airbus crash in the Rhine last year." Grumbling about being left out of the best part of the story, he slid a cigarette from his pocket and lit it. "Bloody Yank prima donna."

The chartered helicopter was already at five hundred meters and heading west when Cannell ducked his head into the EC120's small flight deck and tapped the pilot on the shoulder. "Watch for a couple of Blackhawks. It's part of the official search. I want you to stick to them but not too close."

While his videographer set up for a good view out the open starboard door, Cannell got on the phone to talk with Tanner. He was grinning. "That sanctimonious limey won't be first on this story," he muttered as the connection was made.

"There they are," the co-pilot said, pointing.

Cannell ducked to see out the windshield and saw a small black dot coming toward them from the ridgeline, followed by another. The two helicopters swept past them at full speed. Cannell nudged the pilot to follow. After ten minutes, the Nachtfalkes slowed and separated until they were about five kilometers apart. "They're starting a search pattern," the pilot said to Cannell. "Probably visual, but I'm sure they are using magnetic detectors too."

"Why are they starting so far to the south?" Cannell asked.

The pilot said, "That battle was over three hours ago. I suppose the men you're all looking for are at least fifteen kilometers south by now. The choppers will work their way from there." Then he pointed at the fuel gauge. "We have about an hour's fuel remaining. Just FYI."

Cannell nodded irritably. "I hear you."

For the next twenty minutes, they filmed the two German aircraft as they systematically searched the forest below.

"They seem to be in no hurry," said Aaron Moss, the videographer.

"Jesus Christ," Cannell said after watching the twin black helicopters fly with agonizing slowness over the forest. "This could take all day. We're not getting any good visuals, and we'll lose the daylight in a few hours."

Moss nodded, keeping his eye against the rubber cup of the digital camera. "We might run out of fuel before that, Jason."

"I want first crack at these Romans, whoever they are. We'll follow those choppers for another fifteen minutes, then go back to refuel. When we get back, we'll strike out on our own search. We might get lucky." He grinned wolfishly. "Then Professor Arthur Morley, Ph.D., can kiss my ass for a change."

"We're all set, Al," Rabble said. "The army's giving us a car, and I've got the landing zone in my GPS. Let's go while we can."

"Right." Braden ran over to Ann, beside Sharon, helping her take more blood and tissue samples from another Roman body. Her outfit was rumpled with stains under the armpits, but to Braden, she looked magnificent. "I gotta go, honey. Will you be okay here?"

Ann pursed her lips and blew a skein of sweaty hair from her face. "Some bloody fun holiday you dragged me on, Alexander Braden. Instead of a nice day at a rally with music and food, I'm stuck with a lot of smelly Roman stiffs, playing grave robber." She tried to act mad, but he saw through it.

"Consider it training for a new career in the exciting field of archaeology," he said, kissing her. "Besides, I didn't drag you here. You insisted on coming."

"I'm a loony," she said, returning the kiss. "I'm counting on you to do the right thing. I'll stay with Sharon, and we'll catch up with you later."

"I'll do my best." Then with a wave at Sharon, he ran off to join the other men in a car provided by Colonel Koll. "Let's get cracking," he said, pulling the door closed.

Sergeant Dorfman turned the BMW and headed west down the hill away from the scene of carnage.

CHAPTER VII

NOWHERE TO RUN

Captain Else Klein checked her watch as she saw the news chopper turn east and disappear. "Those reporters don't have much patience, do they?" She looked to her left. "Let's go, Lieutenant. We have an appointment, and I don't want to be late."

"Co-pilot's airplane," Roebach said as he took the controls. "Descending to fifty meters."

The Nachtfalke banked sharply to the north and flew low over the treetops as she pulled her map book from the pocket by her seat and examined it. "Stay with the B27 until we reach the next valley."

Half an hour later, Klein confirmed their location with the GPS and motioned to Roebach. "This is it. Take us down." In her peripheral vision, she saw the other helicopter also slowing in preparation for landing.

Below them was a broad clearing of open fields. It was more than large enough to accommodate the choppers. Just off a nearby road was a BMW military staff car, and beside it stood four men. When the wheels were solidly on the soil, Klein jumped out of the right-side hatch, not bothering to remove her helmet.

"Herr Braden," she said, keeping her head below the deadly arc of the rotors, "shall we go?"

"Yes. What about the press helicopters?"

Klein laughed. "They got bored watching us. It only took about half an hour." She pulled open the huge sliding door and retrieved three flight helmets. She handed one each to Braden, Rabble, and Morley and showed them how to use the boom microphone. "Just hit that small switch on the cord when you want to talk."

Morley put the heavy helmet on. "This is rather out of my line, you know."

"Herr Morley," Klein said with a wide smile and a hand on his forearm, "don't worry. I will give you a very interesting and pleasant ride."

Morley nodded. "That's exactly what I'm worried about. You see, I've never been in a helicopter before."

She grinned, leading him into the open side hatch. "You'll be fine." She introduced Horn and Altmann to Morley as she strapped him into one of the bulkhead seats, taking extra time and fussing over him. Morley seemed to relax.

She's flirting with him, Braden thought as he smiled and belted himself with the four-point restraint into another bulkhead seat.

The HS-66 Nachtfalke could hold nearly twenty men seated in folding benches along the sides and centerline. The turbines increased their whine, and Braden watched Rabble climb into the other craft.

"Okay, gentlemen," Klein's voice said from Braden's helmet headset, "we're ready and will be onsite over the search area in about ten minutes. We will have to do one HIFR in about three hours. Horn, get your video systems up and running. Altmann, power up the MAD and infrared gear."

The two men at the consoles acknowledged the orders.

"Hifar and mad?" Morley said, forgetting to hit the button.

Braden saw his lips move and used his own microphone. "You need to hit that switch to talk, Arthur. Hifar. It's H-I-F-R, for Helicopter In-Flight Refueling. A tanker aircraft will rendezvous with us to fill our tanks. It's a lot of fun to watch." In truth, Braden hadn't ever seen it for real. He didn't want the old professor to become nervous at the sight of a large aircraft flying only a few meters ahead of the HS-66 with the spinning rotor blades seemingly ready to slice the refueling hose like a Cuisinart. "MAD is the magnetic anomaly detector. They can detect the metal in the legionary armor."

"Can they do that from up here?" Morley asked, keying his microphone.

Klein answered for him. "Yes, Professor, we can. At this altitude, we can cover a lane four hundred meters wide. Our MAD gear is set to find any metal object, including a beer can."

I didn't think the Germans used beer cans, Braden thought irreverently.

"Niner-Three, Seven-One," Klein said, "we are beginning our search. Maintain your separation. We are moving up the eastern valley."

It was late afternoon as the surviving legionaries marched through the thick trees. Lucius figured the sun would set in another four hours. The night would come as a welcome relief, a cloak of darkness to keep them safe and hidden. He planned for the men to rest and eat at dusk for a few hours before moving on. He wanted to be far away from the place of the massacre.

Massacre? Was that what they'd left behind? A place of death and savagery?

Not to him. It was a place of restored honor and glory. But to the Germans, it would always be a place of national shame.

In the few hours since they'd left the road and the pitiful few Germans, six more legionaries died on the march. Four had fallen from wounds, the others from the mysterious ailment. It would have taken too long to bury them, and secrecy was no longer important. Each dead man was laid out straight with his hands folded over the gladius on his chest, his shield covering the body like a scarlet wooden shroud. Then the rest moved on, marching north.

Braden watched the endless dark green carpet of the Westerwald pass below the helicopter. He was tired but never took his eyes off the terrain. He was sure they'd find the Romans. Fifty kilometers farther north, the forest ended at a vast open plain of farmland. Time wasn't on the side of the legion, but neither was it on that of the searchers.

Europe and the world had heard of the massacre just west of Chancellor Hoffman's pro-NATO rally. An enterprising journalist had found a roster of Gebirgsjäger Battalion 232 and started calling relatives. This, of course, had resulted in panic among the loved ones, and the lack of solid answers from the Landespolizei or the Defense Ministry provided fertile ground for rumor and misinformation.

Braden heard a call on the Nachtfalke's radio. "Seven-One, Niner-Three. We have something on the ground, zero-two-five degrees. We are transmitting the image. Over."

Klein replied, "Roger, Niner-Three." On the intercom, she said, "Horn, put up the transmission from Niner-Three."

"Got it," the sergeant said. He adjusted a few knobs while Braden and Morley watched the screen. It showed treetops in the foreground, and beyond that was a narrow clearing, perhaps ten meters wide. Lying prone on the ground was a human body under a red-and-gold shield.

"That's them!" Morley said, again without hitting the button. But Braden heard it anyway.

"How long has he been there?" Braden asked. "Can we find out?"

Sergeant Altmann spoke up. "They have an infrared reading. Assuming a lower-than-normal body temperature, and with the ambient air and ground levels, I estimate he's been there for less than an hour."

"They can't be much farther ahead of us," said Braden. He tapped Altmann's shoulder. "Can you do an infrared scan of the area? To find their trail?"

The sergeant began working his console while talking to Sergeant Bayer on the other helicopter. "There is a faint reading farther up that narrow gully beyond where the body is. Heading is 295 degrees. Very weak but it's there."

Braden nodded. "Good enough for me. Captain Klein, can you follow Sergeant Altmann's readings?"

"Copy that," Klein said, and the Nachtfalke banked to the northwest.

Centurio Remus Draconius was the last surviving officer. He was devoted to Lucius and proud to be in Legio LIV. He was last in line and kept an eye on the tiny band of weary, marching legionaries ahead of him. They were just emerging from an area of dense forest with rocky escarpments to their right when he stopped for a moment and cocked his head. Frowning, he pulled off his helmet and cupped his left ear.

There it was again. A faint rhythmic thumping noise far behind them. As he turned, he realized it was growing louder. "Sire!" he called out. "It is back! The flying vehicle! I hear it behind us, getting closer."

Lucius, who had been at the head of the small column, ran back to where Draconius was standing. The legatus took off his own helmet and nodded. "Yes, I hear it too. They are coming."

"What are your orders, Sire?" Draconius had his gladius out and ready.

"We cannot fight one of those flying vehicles. But if we can get the Germans inside them to come out, we can attack them. Get the men hidden in the brush. Use the pine branches and loose soil."

"If they come to find us, they will die like the other barbarians," said Draconius in a firm voice.

The legatus smiled at the other man's optimism. There was no point in dampening it with the cold truth. Draconius ordered the men to spread out and take cover. Lucius watched them pull out their well-used entrenching tools and hastily dig shallow pits to hide in. They'd been doing it for two weeks and had learned well. In minutes, the last remains of the legion disappeared into the soil of Germania.

Only Lucius stayed in the open, waiting, watching, and listening. The sound of the airborne pursuer grew louder. But he would not hide. The time for running and skulking about had passed for Lucius Cassius Aquilius.

"Seven-One, Niner-Three. We see a man standing out in the open about a kilometer ahead. In that clearing past that rocky escarpment. Over."

Klein responded, "Copy, Niner-Three, moving in on your starboard side. Don't see him yet. Please describe. Over."

"Sending you the take from our cameras, Seven-One," said the voice over the radio. "He appears to be alone. He's wearing armor. Over."

Braden glanced at Morley, whose eyes were wide. The radio conversation continued. "He's not running away, but I'm sure he sees us. Have you got our video feed? Over."

"Got it," said Horn. "Zooming in."

Braden and Morley bent closer to peer at the screen. "God," Braden said in a whisper. The image was sharp. Standing there in the clearing was a Roman officer. The man appeared to be about thirty-five years old, with a sharp nose and deep-set eyes. He wore elaborate armor, and the tattered remains of a red cloak hung from his shoulders above his folded arms. The helmet glinted in the low yellow sun and had a wilting crest of red horsehair. He looked directly at them and showed no sign of fear.

"I think that's Lucius," Morley said hoarsely. "It's got to be."

"Probably," Braden agreed. "He's watching us."

"But what about the others? Are they all dead?"

Braden was about to speak when Klein's voice cut in. "What do you want us to do, Herr Braden?"

Braden made a snap decision. "We need to land. But not too close. Is there a good spot farther ahead?"

Roebach pointed to the north. "There, about three hundred meters ahead is a clear spot."

"Looks good," Klein said and keyed the radio. "Niner-Three, Seven-One. We will land at that clear spot about three hundred meters ahead. You orbit overhead, but not too close. Over."

"Seven-One, understood, we will orbit at one klick. Over."

"Seven-One out." Klein took the controls, and the nose dipped, headed for the landing zone.

Lucius watched the two black machines in the sky. They had stopped. The beat of noise assaulted his ears. He saw faces under black helmets looking at him. "You have found us at last," he said to the two flying vehicles. "Come and do what you will. We are ready."

He felt no fear and folded his arms as he stood watching the machines hovering over the trees. He knew his men were watching his every move. They would charge on his order. But he had no intention of giving that order. He wanted to see his enemy face-to-face, to meet the men who had been hunting the legion for so long. It was time to face his barbarian foe and spit in his eye.

Just then, the black flying machine moved. The nose dipped as if it were sniffing for his scent, then it went over him in a roar that made him blink from the storm of dirt and pine needles.

The HS-66 settled down in the wide clearing. Klein shut down the engines. "Altmann, you come with me. We will accompany Herr Braden and Professor Morley. Take your sidearm." Then she took off her helmet and faced Roebach. "Werner, you and Horn stay here. Have Niner-Three keep the video feed on us at all times. If you see anything suspicious or dangerous, call us at once."

"Yes, Captain," the lieutenant said, following her into the main cabin.

When they were standing beside the big helicopter, Klein faced Braden. "I suppose it is your show, gentlemen. Altmann and I are armed, but we don't know how those men will react."

"Neither do we," Braden admitted. His mouth was as dry as dust. He tried to swallow. "But we have to try and talk to them."

"Then lead off," she said, pointing to the south.

With Braden and Morley in the lead, they walked into the thicket of trees surrounding the clearing. Klein was on her radio. "Niner-Three says the man has not moved. He's still standing there."

"Well, Arthur," said Braden in what he hoped was a lighthearted tone, "I guess we'll find out if your Latin is up to scratch."

Morley gave him a weak grin. "It had better be, Alex. But I don't mind saying I'm bloody terrified."

"You and me both, pal." The air was tinged with the scent of pine and moist soil. The trees were dense and tall, cutting off the late-afternoon sunlight. Klein and Altmann walked well away from them, looking all around for any sign of danger. They could almost feel eyes upon them.

Then the trees thinned out, and blue sky appeared overhead. The four people emerged into a small clearing about the size of a basketball court, studded with boulders and thick undergrowth.

With a cold shock, Braden stopped in his tracks. He stared at the man watching them from twenty meters away.

"*Qui ci sono dei Romanii,*" Morley whispered just loud enough for Braden to hear.

Here there be Romans, Braden thought.

The two German aviators also stopped but stayed quiet.

"What do we do now?" Morley asked.

"Let's go and introduce ourselves," Braden said.

They slowly approached the Roman. Time itself came to a stop. *Holy shit,* Braden thought. *This is real.* Before him stood a citizen of ancient Rome, a man who'd served under Emperor Augustus and fought for the Roman Empire. Between them were five meters in space and two thousand years in time. The man's elaborate armor was clean and almost polished. His helmet, reflecting the late-afternoon sky, shielded his eyes under the thick brow guard. A gladius hung at his waist. Then Braden noticed the streaks and spatters of dried blood on the man's arms and armor. German blood.

Braden inhaled deeply and leaned over toward Morley. "Tell him what I say, okay?"

"I'll do my best," Morley said.

Clearing his throat, Braden tried to smile. But the cold, emotionless look on the Roman's tired and drawn face stilled it. Braden pointed to himself. "Uh, I am Alexander Braden."

The Roman's eyes narrowed. Then he licked his lips. "Alexander?" He peered at Braden without saying anything else. Then he turned his dark penetrating gaze on Morley. "What is your name?"

"I am Arthur Morley. A scholar. I come from Britannia, where Gaius Julius Caesar reigned."

The Roman looked at him curiously. "You know of Gaius Julius Caesar?"

"Yes," Morley said with a nod. "I am a teacher and have knowledge of the Empire. We have been looking for many days to find you and your gallant legion."

This seemed to confuse the man even more. "You are not Germans?"

"No," Morley said, shaking his head. "I and my friends are not here to harm you." Then he told Braden what had been said.

"Good thinking," Braden said. "Can you ask him his name?"

Morley said, "May I ask your name?"

The man stood straighter. "I am Lucius Cassius Aquilius, Legatus Legiones of Legio Fifty-four Vindicta in the Army of Emperor Gaius Augustus."

Even though Braden's knowledge of Latin was far below that of Morley, he had no trouble understanding every word. His knees grew weak. "Oh, my God."

Lucius's eyes turned to him. "And you? Alexander? The great general from Macedon who in ages past conquered the known world before the Empire rose from the banks of the Tiber?"

Braden silently wished he had a less historically significant name. He spoke slowly so Morley could translate. "I am named for him. I have come a long way to find and talk with you. How may I address you? By your name?"

The Roman said, "You may call me Sire, as befits my rank, Alexander."

"Thank you, Sire. Can you tell me, are you the only man left of your legion? Are there no more survivors?"

After hearing Morley's translation, Lucius gave him a knowing smile. "I am one of the few left. They are all about us." He waved his hand, and suddenly the ground erupted all around them in bursts of soil and pine needles. Two dozen men stood, all holding swords and spears.

Klein and Altmann dropped to their knees, ready to fire, but Braden yelled. "No! It's okay! Keep your weapons down. Please."

The two Germans lowered their guns but not their guard.

Lucius gave Braden an appraising look. "You are brave, Alexander. You could have my legionaries killed in moments. But you do not. This impresses me. You are no barbarian."

Braden listened to Morley's translation. "Sire, we want to help you. The battle you fought on the road is over, and nothing can be done to change it. You have waited so long to avenge your fallen in the legions of Varus."

Lucius showed his surprise. "You know of our cause? The massacre of the legions under Publius Quinctilius Varus?"

Morley spoke for Braden. "We do, Sire. We learned you had slept for a long time in the cellar in Gallicae to come back to the world to kill the barbarian tribes under the traitor Arminius. It is history to us. You and your brave legion are to be honored for your deeds and devotion to Rome."

The Roman officer seemed to ponder this. "Rome. So much time has passed. What of the Empire?"

Braden asked Morley what was being said. Morley told him. "He wants to know about the Roman Empire."

"Shit. I was afraid of that."

"He deserves to know, Alex."

Braden nodded. "Tell him the truth." He held his breath for Lucius's reaction.

Morley looked at Lucius. "Sire, much has changed in the last twenty centuries. Rome is still the capital of Italia, but the Empire you knew is gone, for over a thousand years. The great civilization you remember is no more, but it has left a legacy of civilization we still revere to this day."

Lucius let a full minute pass before he replied. Then he nodded. "I have suspected this, in this world of noise, lights, armored carts, and flying craft. My world, the world we left behind when we began the Somnum, is gone, and no one ever knew of our sacrifice."

Braden thought Lucius was more resigned than sad. "Sire," he said slowly, "we will see to it you will return to tell the story yourself." He noted the astonishment on Morley's face before he translated.

The Roman's eyes glinted in a sadly amused look. "Do you, Alexander? Do you think the Germans will allow that? We are few invaders in the land of many, many times our number. There is no returning to Rome for us. Even if the Empire still existed, we would never reach it alive. That is why we chose to head to where our journey began." He looked toward the northern sky where the first faint tinges of purple light painted the dusk in the east.

"You are going back to the forest where your legions fell two thousand years ago, Sire?" Braden asked him.

"We are," Lucius said sadly. "I do not know if my men can reach it. The journey is long, and we are weaker by the hour." Then he stopped. "How do you know where we are going?"

Morley replied for Braden. "It was I, Sire. I knew Gallicae held no reason for you to return, nor was there a reason to go to Rome, so far away. To lie among your fallen comrades is all that is left to you."

"Yes," Lucius said, seeing the men around him. "Lower your arms, my legionaries. These men are not our enemies."

Without any protest, the Romans around them relaxed and slid the swords into their scabbards. Braden was relieved and saw the emotion mirrored in the faces of the two Germans. He waved them to come closer. Klein came over, holstering her pistol while Altmann stood nearby. But the sergeant's eyes watched the Romans warily.

Klein whispered to Braden, "I hope you know what you are doing."

Braden showed her a half smile. "So do I." He faced Lucius. "Sire, I would like to introduce two members of the German military, Captain Else Klein and Sergeant Altmann."

Lucius peered at the Germans with curiosity. Then his eyes widened. "You are a woman. A woman warrior? No woman ever carried the banners for Rome."

Klein clenched her jaw, then nodded. "Yes. There are many women in the German military. I am an officer, a . . ." she broke off, looking to Morley for help. "What is my rank in the Roman Army?"

"She is a lower-ranking centurion, Sire," the archaeologist told Lucius. "And the sergeant is probably what you would call a tessararius."

But Lucius was not looking at Altmann. He could not take his eyes off Klein. Even with the baggy flight suit and sweaty hair, it was impossible to miss her beauty. A smile broke over his face, and his voice softened. "I wish to apologize to you. I meant no insult. I have not seen a woman since before we began the Somnum."

Klein smiled too. "I am not insulted."

"I have a request to make of you," Lucius said, looking directly at her. "I wish to speak to a legatus of your army."

Klein showed incomprehension even after hearing Morley's translation. "What is a legatus?"

"A legion commander," Braden said. "The equivalent of an . . . er, division commander, like a general."

"Why do you wish to speak to a legatus, Sire?" Morley asked Lucius directly.

The Roman said, "It is important that we inform your military of what we have done. I want to tell a legatus of the reasons we returned to Germania."

Klein was about to reply when her radio chimed for attention. "Pardon me," she said as she clicked it on. "Klein here."

It was Roebach. "Captain, what is your status? Over."

"We are fine, Werner. Do you have anything to report?"

"Niner-Three is running low on fuel. They need to tank in an hour. Also, I just heard from air traffic control that the news helicopter has landed. They may have discovered the ruse. It won't be long before they find us. Over."

Braden tapped Klein on the shoulder. "I have an idea. Can we talk for a moment?"

"Stand by, Werner," she said into the radio while Braden told Morley to ask Lucius if they could have a moment to talk privately. The Roman nodded and went over to his men.

Braden turned to Klein and Morley. "These men are dying out, and I want to help them. We have to get them out of here. There is only one place they want to go."

"Where is that?" Klein asked.

Morley told her. "The Teutoburg Forest in Lower Saxony."

Her hazel eyes widened. "What? Why there?"

"I'll explain later," Braden said. "Can you get us some trucks from the army?"

The German officer looked at the small band of Romans. "We don't need trucks. We can take all of them there with both helicopters."

Braden stared at her. "Huh? You want to use the helicopters?" He hadn't even considered this.

She shrugged. "Why not? Obviously you want to get them there fast, and I was told to do whatever you needed. The orders I received from General Worden still stand. I will carry them out."

"You know," Braden said sincerely, "they aren't really enemies of Germany?"

Klein nodded. "I understand they did our country a great service, if that's what you mean."

Braden glanced at the small knot of Romans. "Lucius wants to talk to a senior officer. We can call General Worden and have him meet us there." He pointed at her radio. "Can you call the general on that?"

She shook her head. "No. Only my crew. I can call General Worden from my ship."

Braden got a nod from Morley, who had been listening. "That's great. Let's go and tell Lucius that he and his men will be taking a helicopter ride." Then he smiled at Klein. "They already have helmets."

"Aaron, I think that old Limey fart conned me," said Jason Cannell to his videographer as he drank his beer. They sat in a small gasthaus in Wetzlar, a place full of Germans. He and Aaron Moss were the only Americans. The helicopter was not permitted to fly at night, so all Cannell could do was wait until daylight and resume the search.

"No doubt about it," said Moss as he took another pull on his own beer. "We never saw another sign of those Kraut Blackhawks or even an army jeep south of the massacre site."

Cannell glared at him. "You figured that out? You never said anything."

"Not my job. I'm just the guy who points the camera. You're supposed to find the story."

"Smartass," Cannell said acidly. "Well, the story's not here." He finished the beer and ordered another one from a passing waitress. "Shit, Aaron, somewhere out there are a bunch of lunatics dressed up like Roman legionaries who attacked and killed hundreds of Bundeswehr soldiers. And no one is looking for them. Does that make any sense at all? Military and government communication lines should be melting, but here it is, eight hours after the massacre, and the military spokespersons aren't saying shit. No new information, no comments, no leaks. Nothing." He took another long swig. "What did I miss? I've never been wrong."

Jason Cannell was one of the new breeds of television journalists who'd cut their professional teeth on the scandal over the 2016 presidential election. He never read the newspaper, believing the future of journalism was digital. The last six presidential administrations had given the world media a taste for political blood and sensationalism. Up till now, Cannell had been successful at finding the big story. But this time, his journalistic nose had failed him.

"And then I let that old fart lead me off the trail," he muttered. "What the hell was he doing there? A British archaeologist at a German murder site, for Chrissakes. He's about as useful as tits on a bull."

Moss smiled. He liked watching Cannell get himself riled up. "He put on a good show, didn't he?"

"Yeah, and another thing. That fat cop, Schroeder. What was he doing there? An attack on a German Army unit is out of his jurisdiction." With each beer, the reporter was getting more agitated. He'd put in a long day wasting his and the network's time. Atlanta was pissed, Bonn was pissed, and he had nothing to show for it but some boring footage of a roadblock and an interview with a cop who refused to provide any hard facts. "What have I missed?"

Moss put down his beer. "Jason, what happened to those Blackhawks? Where did they go?"

Suddenly Cannell's eyes snapped open. "That's it! Goddamn it! I knew I'd forgotten something." He pulled his phone from a pocket and called a number from his contact list. "Glenn, it's Jason. Listen up. I need something fast. Call the airfield in Koblenz and see if you can get any info on where those Nachtfalke helicopters are now. Find out if any civil airfields have received flight plans from that squadron in the last twelve hours. They have to land somewhere, and they might not be using military fields . . . Just call someone who can find out. It's public record. Call me back as soon as you get something . . . Yes, now. Your beauty sleep can wait." He finished his beer and paid the check. "Let's go. I need to think."

CHAPTER VIII

CAMPFIRE STORIES

Karl Schroeder entered the command trailer. It was quieter than it had been earlier that morning. Only one dispatcher was on duty, and General Worden was talking on a phone.

Ortmann was out coordinating with her people and the park and local police. The park was still on alert, and all the roads out, save the A60, were jammed with vehicles as the public left the site.

Chancellor Hoffman and his party were on their way back to Berlin. The Defense Ministry alerted every German Army unit, both active and reserve. The regional civil defense headquarters were ready to deploy. All across the country, men and women waited for orders. But the complete news blackout started by Schroeder was doing its job. Only certain trusted government members and civil authorities knew the whole story.

Schroeder walked over to the coffee pot and poured himself a cup of strong black coffee. It had been brewed hours before and was now bitter, but he needed the caffeine. Leaning on the map table near a window, he watched Worden. He noted that the normally calm and reserved officer seemed agitated.

"I never gave Klein any such orders," Worden barked into the phone. "Why the hell is she taking the Romans to the Teutoburger Wald? That's up in Saxony near Osnabrück! They're supposed to be under arrest, not receiving a military escort to some old battlefield!"

Schroeder smiled to himself. He felt a lot better than he had that morning. Learning that his nephew was safe and a terrorist group had been destroyed had put him in a good mood. But one thing remained to be done. He took another sip and listened to Worden.

"I don't care if that's what Braden asked her to do. These Romans attacked a Bundeswehr troop column and killed hundreds. They have to be taken into custody." Then Worden turned and saw Schroeder listening. He glared at the police official. "I'll be with you in a moment, Schroeder. I have a crisis."

You do indeed, General, Schroeder thought. "I'll wait." He grimaced at the sour coffee.

The general looked at the wall map. "Where are they now?" His left index finger slid up the map to a location in the northern Westerwald. "Twenty kilometers north of here? For how long? At daybreak? I want to talk to Captain Klein. Put me through to her at once."

A moment later, Worden said, "Captain Klein. This is General Worden. I want to know what you think you're doing, transporting men who are responsible for the murder of hundreds of German soldiers to an old battlefield. They need to be in custody."

After listening, the general spoke again. "I don't care what my orders were. You were to find the Romans and report their location. But you are taking it upon yourself to fly them to Osnabrück. You do not have the authority to make that decision. And Braden is not your commanding officer." He paused again. "They want to what? Why me?" Then he sighed. "Very well. I'll get a plane to take me there. But you, your squadron commander, and I will discuss your actions and decisions at a later time, Captain. I will meet you there in the morning." He slammed the handset down. "Unbelievable."

"Is anything amiss, General?" Schroeder asked innocently.

The general swung to face him. "I would say so. Our revered Herr Braden and the professor have decided that, rather than take the surviving

Romans to a secure location for interrogation, they will fly them to the site of the battle they fought and lost two thousand years ago."

Schroeder expected the general to continue, but evidently, he wanted to hear the Landespolizei official's opinion. "I see," he said, taking another sip. Braden had predicted this, and ever the Romantic, had convinced Klein to help. Schroeder couldn't blame Worden for his reaction. He really did not know the whole story. In fact, Schroeder had made sure of it. "That *is* interesting. And what did Captain Klein also tell you?"

Worden stared at him, surprised at the blasé reaction. "The Roman commander wants to talk to me. A senior Bundeswehr officer."

"Ah," Schroeder said. "So you are going to go to the Teutoburger Wald?"

"Yes," Worden said. He gave an irritated shake of his head. "I seem to have no choice. Apparently, the Romans are rapidly dying out, and time is short. If I wish to confront these men, I have to go to them."

Schroeder nodded. "That NATO jet you arrived in is still at Wetzlar Flughafen. We can use that."

"We?" Worden seemed taken aback. "Why would you go? This is not a Landespolizei matter. It is a military matter."

"Need I remind you," Schroeder said dryly, putting down the cup and crossing his arms, "these same Romans who attacked the army column have also entered the country illegally, killed German citizens, hijacked a towboat, started fires, and stolen livestock. All in my district. I have jurisdiction as well as you. More, in fact."

The army officer considered this. He was clearly unhappy to have the redoubtable Schroeder along, but he could not counter the police officer's logic. "Very well, Schroeder. I will make the arrangements to leave at dawn. Can your people handle things here in your absence?"

Schroeder repressed a smile of triumph. "I believe so. I'll be ready to go at dawn." Then he went over and picked up another phone and made a call. "This is Schroeder. I need to speak with Klaus Becker at the Landespolizei Lower Saxony regional headquarters. Yes. I'll wait." He watched Worden talking on another phone. Then he heard a familiar voice come on the line. "Hello, Karl, how are you? I hear you've had some excitement down your way."

"You might say that, Klaus," he replied. "It's been a madhouse down here. But I need a favor from you."

"Name it, Karl," said the man on the phone.

Schroeder explained for a full minute.

"I can arrange that," Klaus Becker said. "It will be set up when you get here."

Schroeder thanked him and hung up. He turned to leave the trailer. He didn't want Worden to see the broad smile on his face. It was all coming together. He couldn't wait.

"Well, that was interesting," Klein muttered as she stepped out of her helicopter and walked over to where Braden and Rabble were talking. "General Worden will meet us at the site in the morning."

"How did he take it?" Rabble asked.

The German officer bit her lip and looked away. It appeared as if she were trying not to laugh. "He was not happy. He as much told me that I was going against his orders by taking the Romans to Osnabrück. But he'll be there."

"I'm sorry if this is going to be a problem for you," Braden said.

She waved it off. "I'm not worried. General Worden is not my commanding officer. He can threaten but not really do anything to me." She glanced at her watch. "2120 hours. If we take off at 0430 hours, we can be in Osnabrück at 0700. We don't have to land at the airport, but I do have to file a flight plan to Osnabrück."

"Can't we go sooner?" Braden asked. "I'm worried about the press finding us."

Klein pulled a canteen from her belt and took a drink. "I am too, but my crews need rest and food. It's already getting dark. We'll be hard to spot in any case."

Braden and Rabble looked at one another, then at the distant group of Romans in the tree line. "I understand, Captain," Braden said. "We'll do it your way."

"Call me Else," she said, smiling. "First things first. I think we need to help our Roman passengers adapt to the idea of flying."

Rabble chuckled. "That should be fun to watch." He followed Klein and Braden over to where Morley and Altmann, now accompanied by Roebach, Horn, and the crew of the other helicopter, were standing. They turned at Klein's approach. "Okay," she began. "We stand down for the night. Lieutenants Haase and Roebach will see to the preflight at 0330. Takeoff at 0430. I'll have a tanker meet us at 0500. Then we head to the Teutoburger Wald." She motioned to Morley. "Professor, can you help me talk to the Romans?"

"Of course," he replied with a smile.

Lucius and Draconius were talking while the other Romans stood nearby. The legatus turned when he saw Klein and Morley approaching. "Ah, Centurio," he said, looking at her. "What news do you bring?"

Klein smiled at her new rank, then told Morley what she intended to do. "Sire, we will take you and your men to your destination. We leave at dawn. But I want to help you understand what kind of . . . er, transport we are using." She pointed at the twin helicopters in the clearing.

Lucius's dark brown eyes went wide. "In the flying vehicle? How?" He was genuinely disbelieving.

She held up her hands in a placating gesture. "There is no need for worry. Let me show you." Then she motioned for the Romans to follow her. Despite being awed by the act of meeting and talking to real Romans, Klein maintained the image of a calm officer. She couldn't blame Lucius for his reaction. Men born during the time of Christ would have absolutely no concept of flight. Their entire worldview was two-dimensional. North and south, east and west. But no up and down.

It was funny, she thought as she led the way back to the clearing, how alien that seemed to her. Like all civilized humans, she'd grown up accepting flight as commonplace. But to the Romans, it was probably analogous to being in the sky with the gods. Of being dead. She saw the fear and anxiety in their faces, but by explaining that the rotors worked like birds' wings, she could convey how the helicopter flew. Even so, Morley was hard-pressed to translate her words into Latin.

Finally, Lucius walked up to Klein's ship and touched it, feeling the cold metal flanks. He craned his neck to look up at the long narrow rotor blades hanging over him like black swords. "If this is the means the gods have provided, I will accept their mode of transport. My legionaries will follow your orders."

Braden had been watching and listening. "Okay, that's one hurdle behind us."

Rabble grinned. "Now we'll get to make history again."

"You get used to it," Braden said, shaking his head.

Braden, Rabble, and Morley shared the German field rations of hard bread, dried fruit, and canned stew. The flickering orange light of a small campfire illuminated the faces of the men and woman around it.

It was as normal and strange a night as Braden had ever known. As a boy, he'd gone camping with his family and friends, sitting around a fire, toasting marshmallows, and telling ghost stories. But now, the ghosts had come to the campfire.

Talk about culture shock, he thought. But what he was seeing was even more. It was temporal shock. He was watching two groups of people separated not only by nationality and language but two thousand years in time.

Morley leaned over to Braden, and the younger man saw the excitement in his eyes. "I can't bloody believe what I'm doing! Here I am sitting in a German forest, calmly chatting up a bunch of actual living Roman legionaries!"

Braden grinned at him. "Yes, I know. And where's a video camera when you really need one?"

"This will be the biggest thing since the discovery of Tutankhamun's tomb."

The old man returned his attention to the Romans. It was difficult, having to translate back and forth between English and Latin, but he never slowed down. His translation from Latin was fast and precise. Braden helped the three Germans who did not speak English. It made for a colorful conversation.

Lucius, chewing on a piece of dried meat, said, "Arthurus, I have more to ask. What occurred after we left the surface and buried ourselves? Did the Empire regain control of Germania, and was Arminius brought to justice?"

"Sire," Morley began as he settled himself more comfortably on the soft soil near the fire, "in the years after Clades Variana, as it is known, Caesar Augustus had forbidden any further incursion into Germany and fixed the borders of the Empire at the Rhine River."

"Yes," Lucius said. "I know that. It was a very unpopular decree among many in Rome. I heard talk among Senators, equestrians, tradesmen, families of the slain, and even a high-ranking Pontifex of their disagreement with Augustus's order."

"Is that where it began?" Braden asked. "The beginning of your cause for Vindicta?"

Lucius nodded. "It was, Alexander. I met secretly with many of these men, and we found common ground in wanting vengeance on Arminius and his followers. We intended to sleep for two decades and emerge and attack without warning into Arminius's land."

"But by then, it would not have mattered," Morley said, which made Lucius look at him curiously. "Arminius, whose name in the modern German language is Hermann, tried for a decade to unite his tribes and bring all of them together. It was a noble goal, one which might have had great consequences for the future. But it was not to be. Arminius was assassinated at a council of rival tribes ten years after Clades Variana. Even if you had awakened after only twenty years, he was already dead."

This had an immediate effect on the Romans. Lucius dropped his meat. "He was killed? By his own people?"

Morley nodded. "Yes. At the age of thirty-five. He never achieved the goal of uniting the warring tribes of Germany."

For a long moment, no one spoke, and Lucius looked at his surviving men. "It is justice of a sort," he said with a sad smile. "I do not know what to think. Was our cause for nothing? Did we forsake our world, our time, our lives for no reason?"

Draconius, sitting next to Lucius, spoke up. "Sire, that is not true. The barbarians needed to be destroyed. We have done that. Even if the traitor Arminius had been killed, his people were still to be dealt with."

Braden saw Klein and Roebach exchange glances at hearing the translation, but they remained silent.

Morley continued. "After Arminius's murder, the Germanic tribes began warring with one another, fighting and raiding. They degenerated into worse than what they had been before Rome had come to settle the region, and this was the way it remained for a thousand years. Rome would have had a stabilizing influence." He glanced at Klein and the other Germans. "When Arminius attacked the legions and drove Rome from his land, he lost an ally. Rome had lost Germany, but Germany had also lost Rome."

"How is that, Professor?" Roebach asked, finally speaking up.

"Lieutenant," Morley replied, "Germany would have had roads, commerce, stability, trade, education, a strong government, and prosperity if they had worked with Rome. But they lost all that and lived as a pack of feudal, warring tribes without any unity or order for a thousand years. Instead of one strong central empire in Europe, there were several small, short-lived feudal ones. And I don't think I need illustrate what that led to in the last two hundred years."

Roebach considered this. "All the wars we've fought for the last two centuries were caused by the loss of Roman control in Germany? That's hard to believe, Professor. No offense meant."

The old professor smiled. "None taken. But essentially, that's exactly what it means. The Thirty Years' War, the Franco-Prussian War, World War One, and the collapse of three major empires: Communism, Hitler, and World War Two. They might never have happened." Morley paused to drink from his canteen cup. "Rome was a conqueror, but the lands they pacified prospered. All the nations governed by Rome had a far more positive influence on the advances and stability of Europe than Germany. Your country, Lieutenant, had lost what it might have done great things with."

Klein spoke up. "*Ein wendepunkt der geschichte.*"

Braden saw the confusion on the Roman faces, and Morley translated. "A turning point in history. Arminius did more harm to his people by his actions than he could ever have imagined."

Lucius said nothing. His face was dark. Then he looked at his remaining men, who watched him with hooded eyes. "It may be that our cause was unneeded in our time. But we owed it to the families of the twenty-five thousand who died. That has not changed."

The others seemed to accept this.

Then Lucius addressed Morley. "What of Rome? What remains of the Empire?"

"The world owes a great deal of its best aspects to Rome," Morley began. "Our very system of government, science, law, medicine, trade, and learning were given to us by Rome. That is Rome's true legacy, Sire."

Braden spoke up. "And if you need further proof, consider this. The titles of the German Kaiser and the Russian Czar were both translations of 'Caesar.'"

Roebach and Haase's ears pricked up at that. "I never knew that," Haase said, impressed.

The Roman legatus nodded. "Perhaps we have done the right thing after all. Time has changed everything. I have no anger toward our new Germanic allies," he said, facing the six Germans, who all smiled after Morley translated.

"Nor we with you, Sire," Klein said, speaking for all of them. She held out her hand and took his. "We are all soldiers and do our duty for our country."

Lucius nodded, firmly grasping her hand. "We do. Thank you."

While the Germans went to their helicopters for a few hours of sleep, Morley began asking Lucius about Varus and the German campaign. He knew this was probably his only chance to learn the details of the battle that had fascinated historians for ages. Lucius told him everything he could remember while Rabble used his iPod to record the conversation. What they were learning would undoubtedly change history. Morley asked Lucius about his background and family, which the legatus willingly related.

Braden, even though he did not understand Latin, could tell Morley was excited at hearing firsthand about life in ancient Rome.

As the stars in the east faded in the predawn, the old academician shook his head in wonder. "Remarkable. What a story. I cannot wait to write all this down." Then he said, "I would like to ask you a personal question, Sire."

Lucius turned to him. "Yes, Arthurus?"

"Your name. Lucius of the family Cassia. But how did you earn your honorific of Aquilius? I have been very curious about that."

The Roman chuckled. "Ah, that was a long time ago. A very long time ago. I was a young legionary in Cohort Tertius of Legio Eighteen," he said, looking at the sky. "We were on a campaign in northern Gallicae with Legio Seventeen to quell a Celtic uprising. It was my first time in battle. When the barbarians attacked, the Aquilifer was killed and the barbarian chieftain ran with the eagle standard. I impulsively dashed out from the front rank and killed him and brought the standard back." He shook his head ruefully. "Foolish. It could have led to disaster, but a good friend, Vitellus, spoke up for me. I was given the name Aquilius, the 'savior of the eagle.'"

Morley grinned. "Remarkable. Thank you for telling me, Sire."

Then Klein arrived. "I think it's time we get ready. We are going to preflight the choppers and board." She looked at Lucius. "Sire, my people will get you to your destination safely. I promise you that." Then she turned and walked toward the twin Nachtfalkes.

There were only twenty-four Romans still alive. Even as they prepared to leave, one legionary had fallen over and died without uttering a sound. Another had failed to respond when Lucius called his men together. With a fatalism that surprised Braden, the surviving Romans took their dead comrades into the tree line and laid them to rest under their shields.

"They know, Alex," said Morley. "They know they're all dying."

Braden nodded. "I've never seen anything like it. They're so calm about it."

"I suppose after two thousand years," Morley said while wiping his glasses, "death must seem like a nap after a very long, hard day." The old man smiled and went over to help Klein.

Twelve Romans, including Lucius, were led into Klein's Nachtfalke and shown where to sit. They carried their swords, but the large shields had to be left behind. Morley continued translating as Klein showed them how to sit on the jump seats arrayed along the sides of the ship's main compartment. With obvious trepidation, they allowed themselves to be strapped in, armor and all. Braden, already in his seat near Horn and Altmann's consoles, watched with interest. Rabble was aboard the other chopper where Draconius and the rest of the Romans had already been strapped in. He realized these men had never willingly allowed anyone to bind them. It must have seemed like prison restraints.

Lucius's face was calm, but his hands were never still. He kept fingering the grip of his sword as if needing something familiar to hold on to. Braden smiled at him as Morley, now an old hand at riding military helicopters, sat and buckled. He pulled on his helmet and keyed the microphone. "Can you hear me, Alex? Over, I think."

Braden suppressed the urge to laugh. "Yes, Arthur. Loud and clear. Over."

Klein ducked into the flight deck and sat in the right-hand seat. Her voice came through Braden's headset. "Niner-Three, Seven-One. Start engines. Standard departure. Course is three-four-one degrees, altitude eight hundred meters, speed two hundred knots. We'll rendezvous with the refueling aircraft in two-zero minutes. Over."

"Understood, Seven-One," was the reply from the other helicopter. "Starting up now."

Then Klein turned in her seat. "We're ready to go, gentlemen. Professor, can you tell our passengers we are starting the engines? They will hear a loud whining noise, but it's nothing to be alarmed about." She nodded to Roebach, who began flipping switches and adjusting levers.

Morley leaned toward Lucius, who was sitting closest to him, and explained what was happening. The Roman legatus nodded and passed the word down the line of legionaries. They displayed different reactions. A couple appeared to be close to being sick, and Braden suddenly wondered if they should be issued Barf Bags.

Over their heads, a low hum increased in volume and pitch as the turbines spooled up to takeoff power. Braden saw the long black rotor blades turning just outside the windows. In a moment, their heavy blat hammered at the helicopter's cabin. The ship shook with a rhythmic shudder.

The Romans' faces showed both alarm and interest. Lucius shouted something to them, but Morley shrugged at Braden. He hadn't heard the legatus's words.

A minute later, the helicopter gave a gentle lurch as Klein lifted the collective. The Nachtfalke, burdened with the weight of eighteen men, lifted off into the dawn sky. Braden watched as the trees around them fell away. The forest and mountains spread out to an endless dark green horizon. He glanced at the Romans. They stared out the broad windows as the world dropped away. He noted that they all clutched at the metal seat frames as if they were afraid to let go.

Lucius again shouted something, and this time, Morley keyed his microphone and spoke to Braden. "He said, 'We are in Apollo's chariot and in good hands.'"

Braden nodded, smiling. Lucius had to be just as nervous as his men, but he was a leader. Leaders must never show fear.

The refueling went smoothly. Klein closed the hatch to the flight deck so the men in the rear couldn't see what was happening up front.

Fifteen minutes later, both helicopters were fueled, and they flew north over the rich farmlands and cities of central Germany. Braden checked his watch. It was almost five-thirty. The long odyssey was almost over. For him, it had been only two weeks, but for Lucius and his men, who had seen the passing of entire ages and centuries, it was a lifetime.

A lifetime that was almost over.

Glenn Redmond was on Jason Cannell's ENN support team. Ever since Cannell's call the previous night, Redmond had been on the phone in his Wetzlar hotel room trying to find out where the German helicopters had gone. He wasn't in a good mood. It had at first appeared to be a simple task. But as the hours passed, he was more frustrated. "Goddamn him," Redmond growled, wishing he'd taken the job in Britain with the BBC rather than the higher-paying job with ENN. The pay wasn't enough to compensate him for the lost sleep and to put up with an arrogant asshole like Jason Cannell.

It was almost dawn, and so far, he'd come up dry. The German military was good at keeping secrets. Frustrated, he was about to call Cannell and give him the bad news, but then he heard the whine of jet turbines to the south. His sixth-floor room faced that way, and he stood to look out the window. The eastern sky turned from a gunmetal gray to a rosy violet streaked with creamy clouds. The airport was five kilometers away, and he saw the glint of floodlights on smooth white metal. Then a set of landing and navigation lights winked on, and he recognized the sleek form of a Gulfstream business jet. *Oh yeah,* he thought, picking up a mug of cold coffee. *That NATO jet.* The distant form of the aircraft moved to the western end of the runway. Redmond watched it. He needed a break from the tedium. A moment later, the NATO Gulfstream's engines whined louder, and it streaked down the runway. He followed the tiny red, green, and white lights as the plane climbed steeply into the predawn sky.

A minute later, the jet passed over his hotel. "Going north," he muttered. Going back to the phone, he picked it up and called the Wetzlar airport. He got through to the night shift controller, a girl with a crisp voice named Hilda Rudel.

"Good morning, Fräulein Rudel," he said in his best German. "This is Glenn Redmond with European Network News. I'm sorry to bother you again, but can you tell me what flight plan that NATO jet filed?" It was public information, even in Germany.

"Of course," replied the girl. "I have it here. NATO Gulfstream number GH-67822. Destination is Osnabrück."

Redmond had never heard of it. "Where is that?"

"Lower Saxony."

That didn't help. Redmond wasn't familiar with German geography. "Do you know who was on board?"

"I'm sorry, sir, but I cannot give out that information. I'm sure you understand."

"Yes, of course. Thank you." He hung up and pulled a battered German map book out of his travel bag. After thumbing through the index, he found Osnabrück. "Why would they go there? That's nowhere." He went to his laptop and looked up the Wikipedia entry for Osnabrück. "Not much more than a college town." Then he found a link entitled "Kalkriese Roman Historic Battle Site." He clicked on it and read with increasing interest. "A Roman battle site," he muttered.

He found the number for the Osnabrück airport and got through to another night controller. The man was yawning as he answered. "Osnabrück Flughafen control, may I help you?"

Again, Redmond introduced himself and asked about the NATO jet's flight plan.

"Yes, it was filed a few hours ago," the sleepy voice replied. "ETA is approximately 0720 hours."

Redmond checked his watch. "It just left Wetzlar. Can you tell me anything else?"

"Not really." There was a pause. "We've never had a NATO aircraft come here before, and now we get two in one night."

"Two?" Redmond asked, puzzled. "Two what?"

"Well, about an hour ago, an ETA came in from a military flight."

A tingle went up Redmond's spine. "Military?"

"Two Bundeswehr helicopters."

"Are they coming to the airport?"

"No. They are headed for the archeology site north of the city."

Bingo. Redmond knew he had hit paydirt. "Thank you for your help." *Now you can go back to sleep.* "This should satisfy that asshole," he said with a grin. Then he reached for his phone.

Doctor Sharon Kelly was more tired than she ever remembered being. Even the muted thrum of the Gulfstream's twin engines failed to penetrate her fatigue. But her mind refused to settle. Visions of the massacre site and working on the Roman corpses kept intruding as she tried to relax. Ann Hamilton was sleeping in the seat ahead of her.

Karl Schroeder had found the two women as they entered the Wetzlar police station, and he invited them to join him on the flight. At first, Sharon considered declining. She still had a lot of work to do on the bodies, but when the police official told her there would be live Romans at their destination, she readily agreed. After ensuring that the bodies and samples were in good hands with the local medical examiners, she and Ann went to a hostel to wash up and change before boarding the Gulfstream at five o'clock in the morning.

Sharon continued to puzzle over the mystery of how and why some Romans had died while others continued to live. She needed live Romans, someone she could talk to. In a way, it was like obtaining a verbal medical history instead of running diagnostic tests.

In the seat across from her was the rotund form of Schroeder, sitting two seats behind General Worden. Even through her fatigue, she noted a distinct difference in their behavior. Worden was clearly agitated, while Schroeder slept soundly. Shortly after takeoff, Worden had been on the satellite phone, but after a few minutes, he angrily banged the handset down. Then he stormed into the flight deck. "I need to contact the Defense Minister immediately," he said in a voice that carried to the rear of the cabin. "But I can't get a single connection."

The co-pilot said something to Worden that Sharon could not hear.

Then Worden roared, "Do you mean to tell me that there are no working satellite links on this aircraft?"

The other man pointed to something on the complex control console and spoke again.

"I don't care about atmospheric interference," the German general said loudly. "I need to talk to the defense minister in Berlin at once! Fix it now!" Then he stormed out and took his seat.

Sharon noticed that Schroeder, who she thought had been sleeping, was smiling.

I wonder what that's all about, she wondered vaguely. *He looks like the cat that swallowed the canary.*

The sky outside the windows brightened to a clear periwinkle blue tinged with purple. She glanced at her watch. It read 5:45. Just twenty-four hours earlier, she had climbed into this same jet in Brussels. *What a difference a day makes.*

CHAPTER IX

SILVIS HORRIDA

The two black HS-66s flew through clear early-morning skies as they approached the northern German city of Osnabrück. Klein keyed the radio. "Osnabrück control, this is Army Nachtfalke Seven-One, over."

The reply was immediate. "Seven-One, we have you on radar. Your flight plan shows your destination as the Teutoburg battle site. Over."

"That is affirmative, control. Do you have any traffic in the area? Over."

"Negative, Seven-One. But be advised a NATO special flight is also inbound for the airport, ETA two-zero minutes, over."

"Copy that, Osnabrück. Stand by." She keyed the intercom. "Professor, where are we going? Can you show us?"

Morley craned his head around but couldn't see through the narrow door to the flight deck. He undid his harness and stood, leaning forward. "Let me see," he said over the intercom. "There, see that road coming out of the city and bending to the north? The battle site is about twenty kilometers up that road. The hills on the horizon are Kalkriese."

"I see it," Klein responded.

Morley regained his seat and leaned over to speak to Lucius. Braden couldn't hear what he said, but it was easy to guess. Lucius leaned over to talk to the legionary next to him. The other man nodded and passed the word on to the others. To a man, the Romans appeared both anxious and eager. They had borne their first, and probably last, helicopter ride well, but they obviously wanted nothing more than to get their feet back on solid ground.

Then the air traffic controller's voice broke in. "Army Seven-One, you are cleared to go to your destination. Be advised that police officers are waiting for your arrival."

Braden's eyes widened at this, and he exchanged a nervous glance with Morley. *What the hell are the police doing there?* Then he realized that it had to be Schroeder's doing. He had probably arranged for some local police to cordon off the area and keep it clear of civilians.

"Understood, Osnabrück," Klein replied. "Thank you. Proceeding to destination."

The Romans craned their heads to look out the windows as the helicopter banked and headed north. Lucius managed to loosen his harness and was almost standing in order to see. Braden couldn't blame him. For the Roman commander, this was the end of a long, dangerous journey.

Small towns, neat farms, wide cultivated valleys, and meandering gullies passed beneath them. In the distance was a dark forest so thick it appeared almost primeval. The tall pines stabbed into the sky like millions of deadly spears.

The HS-66 slowed, and Morley leaned into the flight deck again. He pointed to the right.

"That's it. See those buildings? That's the visitor center. Beyond it is a large dirt parking lot you can land in."

"Niner-Three, Seven-One," Klein said. "We will land on that field past the buildings, over."

"Roger that, Seven-One," Haase replied.

Klein lowered the collective and pulled back on the cyclic. The HS-66 slowed and flared for landing. A cloud of brown dust and flying grit enveloped the windows. As the helicopter bounced lightly on the landing gear, the turbines' whine droned to a low hum. "We're here, gentlemen," said Klein. "Professor, it's your show now." She pulled off her helmet and ran a hand through her sweaty blonde hair. "I'll go talk to the police while you sort things out here." Then she climbed out of her hatch, followed by Roebach.

Braden heard Morley's voice in his headset. "As you probably know, Alex," the Englishman said, "in 1838, the German government erected a statue of Arminius, called the Hermannsdenkmal near Detmold. The statue is about fifty meters tall. It is a popular tourist site and a place of pride for rabid German nationalists. I do not think it prudent to show the Romans that part of the Teutoburg Forest."

Braden nodded. "I agree, Arthur. We don't want Lucius and his men to see that Arminius is revered in Germany."

Anticipation mingled with dread in Lucius's body as one of the Germans slid the wide hatch open to reveal the broad field. The dust was settling. Beyond the edge of the field was a rising slope of thick brush dotted with pine trees. Past that was a steep ridgeline covered in dark, impenetrable woods. He stood and walked on unsteady legs to the open hatch. He inhaled the morning air, ripe with the smell of soil and dry grass.

"This is the place?" Lucius asked Morley, who stood beside him. "I do not recognize it. The land is too open. The forest is sparse, not as I remember." He gave the Englishman a suspicious look. "Where is the road we marched on?"

"This is the place, Sire," said Morley. "I know it must look very different from what you remember. Farmers and loggers have greatly cut back the forest over the years. The road you traveled on is long gone. The bogs were drained over several hundred years and turned into farmland." He pointed to the east at a wide field of tall corn. "There was a big one right over there." Morley gave the Roman a knowing look. "Trust me, Sire, this is the place where Arminius attacked your legions. Up that trail, archaeologists found several artifacts of the massacre. None were found to the west or north, so this is probably where the last battle occurred."

The legatus regarded him for a long moment, then jumped to the ground. He stood there, eyes scanning the scene around him. *It is different,* he thought. *What is missing? The mud? The bogs and deep black forests?* Walking a short distance into a copse of evergreens, Lucius stopped and looked around him. He inhaled deeply, trying to calm his tortured mind.

"I do not smell blood," he said aloud to himself. "The smell is missing. The smell of death and bloated bodies rotting in the heat. The stink of mud running red with Roman blood is gone." He bent over and clutched a fistful of damp, dark earth. Holding it to his nose, he smelled it. Then a cold chill struck him like a thrown knife in his belly. In an instant, the ages evaporated and time stood still.

It was there. There was no mistaking that stench. The smell of death and defeat and fear was in the soil, even after more than two thousand years.

"I am back," he said, his eyes on the blue morning sky. "By the gods, I have at last returned."

Here the hills had once echoed with marching feet clad in worn caligae, the clanking of armor and pots and canteens. The hot, humid air had been ripe with the scent of wet foliage and mud, the reek of sweat, of dirty hair, of filthy animals hauling packs of moldy food. Long ago, this very forest had harbored thousands of screaming demons in armor and leather waving long swords, yelling in fury as they charged at the Romans. This same ground had hidden them, had sheltered them before they did their deadly work. Lucius saw the swinging swords and thrusting spears, clouds of arrows slicing the air like angry hornets. He watched men, women, and children writhing and screaming in agony in pools of blood and gore, their entrails spilling out onto the thick soil of Germania.

It had been here.

But now it was quiet. The barbarians were long dead. He was the only man in the entire world who had actually seen what had happened here. And soon, he would die, to sleep in eternal peace with his friends. Lucius Cassius Aquilius had finally arrived at his destiny. He felt a wave of emotion sweep through him like a cold tide. It took him several moments to steady his heaving chest and the wild beating of his heart. He rejoined the others and nodded to his legionaries waiting silently on the two helicopters.

"We have come home, my loyal men. Come down. This is the place where our long odyssey began. And where it must soon end."

Braden stepped down and watched the Romans. For the moment, they appeared relieved to be back on the ground. A legionary next to

Draconius bent over and put both his hands palm down on the dark soil. Then he stood with a look of satisfaction on his dirty face.

"Arthur," Braden said to Morley, "I'm going to talk to the police. Can you handle things here for a few minutes?"

The archaeologist smiled at him. "Of course, Alex."

Rabble was unusually quiet as Braden led the way to the edge of the field where a large gray-painted police van was parked. Braden felt the warm morning sun on his shoulders. Klein was talking with a tall, strikingly handsome German police officer dressed in the uniform of the Landespolizei. "Ah, Herr Braden, this is Colonel Abel."

Braden took the man's offered hand and shook it. "Very nice to meet you, Colonel. Were you sent by Karl Schroeder?"

"Indirectly," Abel said. "My orders come from our own district headquarters. We are to cordon off this area and keep any unauthorized persons from entering. We have already stationed men at the entrance and side roads. Others are patrolling the woods and trails." Abel looked the epitome of a German officer, strong and efficient as hell. "If you need anything, my men are at your disposal."

"Are they all Landespolizei?" Rabble asked.

Abel shook his head. "Just myself and two others. The rest are local police. But our orders come directly from Landespolizei headquarters."

Braden let out a sigh of relief. Whatever he'd once thought of Karl Schroeder, he had long since come to respect the man. "Thank you, Colonel. We have some . . . er, foreign visitors, and we're going to take them on a tour of the battle site."

If Abel thought this an odd statement, he didn't show it. "Very well, Herr Braden. I will issue orders to the officers." Giving Klein a smart salute, he walked to the van and picked up the radio.

Klein said, "Do you need us to help with the Romans?" They turned to see Morley leading the Romans along a bordered path that wound its way up the slope past the buildings of the visitor center. They saw him pointing and gesturing as he talked.

"I'm not sure yet," Braden said. "But stand by. We might have to make a quick getaway."

She turned her head to look at him quizzically. "Getaway?"

He gave her a weak smile. "Sorry. I'm just being paranoid. I'm not sure what's going to happen or who will show up and crash the party."

Again she seemed puzzled. Then she laughed. "Oh. I think I understand. Well, if you need to . . . ah, take it on the lam, as you Americans say, my crews are ready."

Then she walked back to the helicopters.

As Braden and Rabble caught up with Morley and the Romans, he heard the Englishman speaking Latin. When Morley saw Braden standing nearby, he said, "Ah, Alex. I was telling them that about thirty years ago, a team of archaeologists from Germany and England were excavating a pit along the base of that ridge there. The remains of a wall that Arminius's men had built to conceal themselves during the attack had collapsed. They found several artifacts underneath it, but the most remarkable find was a bronze cavalry mask."

Lucius frowned for a moment. "I remember that mask. It was worn by . . ." He paused. "Rubius. A cavalry officer. He was vain and obsessed with protecting his face from injury. It was Rubius who rode from the rear to warn of the barbarian attack on the column." His voice was hollow. "I later saw his body crushed under that wall."

Braden watched Lucius as he walked along the trail. The Roman's deep-set brown eyes never ceased their restless survey of the ancient battlefield. His men followed in silence. Soon they entered the tree line and reached a wide dirt path that curved along the base of a steep hill. Up the slope, the evergreens blotted out the mid-morning sun. The air became chill, and even the birds had gone quiet.

Lucius turned on the spot and looked all around him. "I think I know this place." He spoke slowly, and Morley translated to Braden and Rabble. "I think it was here that the barbarians made their final attack." He pointed to the northeast. "Yes. That mountain on the horizon. I recognize it now . . ." Then he spun and looked up the slope into the thick forest. "There!" He pointed at a spot about fifty meters up the steep incline where the soil had eroded to expose an area of bare rock. "That is where the traitor Arminius and his father, Sigimer, stood and watched us being massacred. They stood right there. Sigimer had shouted for his barbarians to halt." His voice shook with emotion and rage. "I saw them looking down on us and the results of their treachery and betrayal. Sigimer and Arminius wanted some of us alive to carry the shame of our defeat forever."

For a long moment, the Roman stared up the slope as if he wished for a way to reach into the depths of time and kill the men who had murdered and slaughtered so many of his friends and comrades. Finally, he took a deep breath. "It is a dark memory I have of this place. Dark, deadly forest, that horrible swamp, the smell, the heat, the blood. A place of death and misery and defeat."

Braden said, "*Silvis Horrida aut paludibus foeda.*"

Lucius looked at him curiously. "Yes. That is exactly what it was."

Rabble asked, "What does that mean?"

Braden said, "Fearful forest and stinking bog. The one began where the other ended. Tacitus wrote it." Any lingering doubt that Braden still held that Lucius was a survivor of the Varian Disaster evaporated. He was sure. The Roman before him had really been here, long, long ago.

Lucius walked slowly along the trail. Underfoot, the soil was soft and moist. The pine needles absorbed the sound of his footsteps. The sunlight disappeared, seemingly sucked into the black canopy overhead. Here were the ghosts of thousands of men and women he'd known and loved. Their restless spirits inhabited the trees and the darkness.

He stopped and sagged to his knees. Then the tears began. In all the years he'd remembered and lost, Lucius Cassius had never openly wept. A wave of powerful sorrow and despair swept into him. The tears streamed down his cheeks, but he felt no shame, only seeing the faces and hearing the voices of his long-dead family and comrades in his mind. He threw his head back, eyes clenched tight, and with a deep breath, howled into the dark trees. The sound echoed from the nearby hill, the moan of a tortured soul, long denied release, screamed from Lucius's lungs in the still morning air.

Then he took a long breath and called out into the sudden silence. "Vitellus! Marius Civilus, Ignus, all of you, I am back among you, my brothers and comrades. Livia, my beloved! You and our son, Cornelius, may at last rest in peace. We have done as we vowed." He raised his fist, shaking it toward the hidden sky. "Oh, Augustus, forgive our duplicity! It is done, and I will soon be with you all!"

At last, Lucius stood and turned to face the others. "It is done. There is nothing left but to await the end." He walked along the line of Roman legionaries and, one by one, clasped their hands warmly. To each, he said, "Thank you for your loyalty, service, and sacrifice. I am proud to have led you. You are truly a soldier of Rome." Then he stepped back and regarded them all. "I only wish we could have taken our triumph back to Rome and rejoined our families. But it was not to be."

For a long moment, the cold trees and dark woods around them were as still as a tomb. Then a loud voice rang out and startled them all.

"These men are under arrest!"

Braden and the others whirled about, stunned to see General Worden striding purposely toward them. He looked both furious and triumphant.

CHAPTER X

COMRADES AND TRAITORS

General Hermann Worden stopped and faced the Romans. His steel-gray eyes glared at Lucius with unconcealed aggression. Lucius looked at Morley and spoke, but the archaeologist didn't translate. Instead, he said something to Lucius, who nodded and waited.

Then Worden faced Morley. His expression didn't change. "Good. You speak Latin. These men are under arrest for capital crimes. You will tell them to drop their weapons and sit on the ground. The police will be arriving to take them into custody."

Just then, Schroeder arrived, panting from running to keep up with Worden. The Landespolizei officer caught Braden's eye and shook his head very slightly. Before Braden could make sense of this, Morley replied to Worden. "I will not tell them that, General. I refuse." He thrust his chin out at the German, whose face turned crimson.

There was no sign of the calm charm Braden had come to associate with Worden. He looked like a man in the throes of apoplexy.

"You refuse?" Worden roared at Morley. "Do you have any idea what this is about? I am here to see these murderers arrested. You are guests in my country. You will tell them what I have to say."

Ann Hamilton came up to Braden. "Are you okay, love?" she said quietly.

Braden's eyes nearly popped from their sockets. "Ann! What the hell are you doing here?"

"Oh, that's a lovely welcome," she said, cocking her head. "Karl gave Sharon and me a lift on the NATO jet."

Braden's brows rose nearly to his hairline. "Karl?"

She giggled. "He's actually quite charming when you get to know him."

"I see," he said slowly. Then he hugged her. "Glad to see you."

Ann looked at the men facing Worden and Morley. "So those are real Romans from thousands of years ago?"

Braden nodded. "Yep. This is the end of their long journey. They came here to die."

Sharon also arrived and went to Morley, who was still facing Worden with a defiant expression. "Hi, Arthur. Is there anything I can do?" She never took her eyes off the Romans.

He looked at her, but before he could speak, Worden interrupted. "Doctor Kelly. Do you speak Latin?"

Sharon answered without thinking. "Yes, I do."

Worden shot a smug look at Morley. "Then you will tell these men what I want them to hear."

Sharon glanced at her mentor, then back at Worden. "I will not. Tell them yourself."

Braden saw the German's jaw drop. *Oh boy, he's about to explode.*

"General," Morley said, "I refuse to tell them anything you have to say. These men have come here to die, not to be arrested."

Worden's eyes narrowed. "If you don't tell them to drop their weapons now, I will order the police to take them by armed force."

"What police would that be?" Morley asked, looking around them. "Other than Commissioner Schroeder, I see no other police officers."

"I spoke to the officers guarding the site. They will be here soon." Worden looked back the way they'd come, but the trail leading back to the landing area was empty. "Schroeder, you go and see what is keeping them."

But the Landespolizei official didn't move. He kept watching Worden with a calculating gaze.

"I don't need you, Englishman," growled Worden to Morley. "I'll make my intentions clear without your help." He stood, directly facing Lucius, who returned his hard stare.

It had to be one of the strangest confrontations in history. *And history is exactly what it is,* Braden thought. The tall, taciturn Worden of the modern German Army in a neat dress uniform and the shorter, dirty Lucius of a long-dead army in the remains of his tattered tunic and weathered armor.

Lucius spoke to Morley. "Arthurus, who is this man who speaks so disrespectfully to you?"

Morley turned to him. "Sire, this is General Hermann Worden, a high-ranking officer in the German Army."

Lucius regarded Worden for a long moment. To Braden, it seemed the Roman commander was not impressed.

But then Worden spoke directly to him. "You and all your men," he gestured to the other Romans, "are under arrest for capital crimes." He pointed to their swords. "Drop those now." His fingertip stabbed down at the ground. "You will not be harmed if you comply at once."

Lucius did not move, but his face showed a growing annoyance. Then he spoke calmly. "You dare give orders to a legatus of the Roman Army?"

Worden whirled on Morley. "What did he say?"

Morley said calmly, "He said, 'You dare give orders to a legatus of the Roman Army?'"

The German almost exploded. "I order you to tell him what I said. Now!"

"You don't have the authority to order me to do anything," the archaeologist replied firmly.

"No?" Worden sneered. "I can have you expelled from Germany and never permitted to return."

Braden spoke for the first time. "For what offense?"

Worden spun to face another adversary. "Failure to cooperate with government officials in the performance of their duty." He was beginning to sound as if he was backed into a corner. "You are all guests in Germany and have no legal status here."

"I have diplomatic immunity, as does Mister Rabble. The professor was invited by Jonathan Howard of NATO. I don't think Chancellor Hoffman would look favorably on us being expelled."

The general's face grew even redder. "Are you threatening me, Herr Braden?"

Braden's own face showed a confidence he didn't feel. "Try me, General. I don't think you want to risk what might happen if your Stormtroopers come in here and try to arrest these men. They've broken some laws, but I don't think that's an issue here. They come from another time, another age. And they'll never understand your actions."

"Enough!" Worden roared. "I don't care if they understand! They invaded my country and killed its citizens. And just yesterday, they attacked and killed over three hundred German troops without mercy."

What the hell is he talking about? Braden was about to reply, but he saw Schroeder shoot him a sharp look that seemed to say, "Please keep quiet."

Worden kept shouting. "These men are criminals and murderers. I don't care where they came from. They killed German troops in cold blood. I want them arrested and will not hesitate to order my men to shoot them if they resist."

It was too much for Morley, and his face showed a mixture of rage and confusion. "Shoot them? What in bloody hell for? They did you a favor. They saved a lot of lives at the rally."

The German's eyes first narrowed, then widened. "What? What are you babbling about?"

"You don't know?" Morley didn't catch Schroeder's attempt to stop him. "Those weren't soldiers. They were terrorists. They were on the way to attack the rally."

If Professor Arthur Morley had thrown a live hand grenade into their midst, he could not have caused a stronger reaction in Worden. The general's mouth fell open. "But that's impossible. They . . . they were following the Gebirgsjäger battalion. It was arranged . . ." Then his voice faded, the echo drifting away in the silence of the dark woods.

Schroeder came to stand in front of him. "Yes, Hermann? You were saying?"

The general blinked several times, then seemed to get control of himself. "I don't know what you're ranting about. But nothing has changed. I am going to place these men under arrest. And if they resist, they will be shot."

"You and what army?" Schroeder said, glancing over to smile at Braden. "I always thought that a useful American phrase. I never had occasion to use it before."

Despite the tense situation, Braden grinned at the police official.

"I told you," said Worden. "Those officers outside the forest. I expected them by now." Then his steel-gray eyes narrowed, peering intently at the police official. "What have you done, Schroeder?"

"Nothing I would regret. Unlike you," Schroeder said with a hard edge to his voice.

"What?" Worden said.

Schroeder reached down and put his right hand on the butt of his holstered Walther service pistol. "Those officers are under my command, not yours. I told them to remain in place."

"You what?" Worden bellowed, the words causing a startled bird to erupt from a nearby tree and fly away in a flutter of wings. "What are you saying, you fat fool? These men are criminals!"

"It takes one to know one," Schroeder said with a raised eyebrow. "It is you that will be placed under arrest."

"What are you talking about?" The tall Worden towered over the stocky Schroeder, but the police official didn't seem the least bit intimidated. "Ever since Herr Braden convinced us of the threat posed to the rally by the Romans, your actions seemed odd. You ordered all the GSG-9 units to deploy to find the Romans. All of them. It seemed a risky move."

"You are not a soldier," Worden replied with scorn.

"Yet my responsibility was to protect the Chancellor and everyone at the rally. From that point on, I kept my eyes on you."

Worden shook his head. "You're the one who fought our efforts to find and stop the Romans in the first place. We in the military were forced to use our own assets."

"I suppose that remains to be seen when the investigation is concluded," Schroeder said.

Worden glared at him. "What did Professor Morley mean when he said the men killed were not Bundeswehr troops but terrorists?"

Schroeder studied the other man. "Why don't you tell me? You were one of them."

Worden reeled back as if he'd been struck. "You're insane!"

Schroeder shook his head. "I found the bodies of two men dressed in Bundeswehr officers' uniforms in the lead staff car. One of them was named Horst Molders, a former captain in the Third Panzer Division based in Cologne in 1999. Then he transferred to an army staff college, where he fell in with some men who had ties to radical anti-NATO factions in the government. Molders shared their view of a racially unified and politically isolated Germany."

"That would be a mistake," Worden said. "Germany needs the ties with NATO and the rest of Europe."

"Spoken like a true NATO supporter," the police official said matter-of-factly. "Molders was later transferred to a staff job in Brussels where he was an aide to a colonel."

The general remained silent, but his eyes showed a hint of fear.

Schroeder raised his eyebrows. "Horst Molders, a man known to be working with groups plotting against NATO, was assigned to the staff of Colonel Hermann Worden, who was on the fast track to earn his general's stars."

"I had several men on my staff," Worden said flatly. "I didn't know anything about their backgrounds."

Schroeder continued. "Molders had called unwanted attention to himself when he spoke out too often about Germany leaving NATO. He made some people in the government nervous. When you were on the brink of general's rank, he resigned."

"What is so suspicious about that?" Worden asked.

"Nothing in itself. But exactly two months later, a bomb was planted at an American supply depot, and seven men were killed. An anarchist group that called itself the New Order of Deutschland took credit for the bombing."

Worden nodded wearily. "I know about that. The Bundeskriminal-amt was hunting them. I fail to see what this has to do with me."

"Two more bombings followed in which more than forty American soldiers and several civilians were killed. Only after the third incident were any arrests made. Six men suspected of being members of the NOD were questioned. One of them was Horst Molders. There wasn't enough evidence to hold them, and Molders and his cronies disappeared after that. As the bombings and protests continued, Chancellor Hoffman made it a priority of the Justice Ministry to find and arrest the terrorists." Then Schroeder paused, and his voice took on a silky tone. "But strange as it may seem, General, every time an arrest was imminent, the culprits always managed to escape without a trace. It was obvious they were being tipped off. The Bundeskiminalamt and Landespolizei investigators were sure it had to be someone high up in the Justice Ministry. But we were unable to find out who was aiding the NOD."

Braden and the others watched the drama unfolding between the two Germans, but no one spoke. Suddenly a wheezing groan made everyone turn to see one of the Romans fall to his knees. The man slid to the dark, cool soil and died, his breath ceasing in seconds.

Sharon moved over and knelt by the man's side. Lucius turned to Morley. "What is that woman doing?"

"She is a physician—a medicus—Sire," Morley said. "She may be able to help you." Morley stood next to Sharon. "That's been happening more and more frequently. Do you have any theories as to why some are still alive?"

Sharon glanced at the two Germans. "I do, but it'll keep."

Lucius frowned. "Arthurus, I demand to know what is happening here. Are these men," he pointed at Worden and Schroeder, "a threat to us? Why are they quarreling?"

Morley leaned close to Lucius and said calmly, "Sire, there is something important happening. I do not know what it is, but I beg you to be patient. I will explain when I can."

"Patience," Lucius said as he looked at the dead man lying on the ground, "is not a luxury I can afford. But I will wait."

"Thank you, Sire." Then Morley told Braden what had just been said.

Worden crossed his arms. "This is becoming tiresome, Schroeder. You have not said why you think I had anything to do with this Molders character."

Schroeder shrugged. "Actually, no one in the Justice Ministry could come up with an explanation. But yesterday, it all came together."

"Yesterday?" Worden asked.

"The other dead man in the staff car was Josef Hauser, a rabid anti-NATO fanatic. When Hauser was a boy, his father was run over by an American tank. He formed NOD and recruited Molders as his security chief."

Worden remained standing with his arms crossed defiantly.

The Landespolizei officer continued. "Next to Hauser on the back seat was a folder containing official Defense Ministry documents for the commanding officer of Gebirgsjäger Battalion 232. They authorized the orders to travel to the rally and serve as Hoffman's honor guard. They were exact duplicates of the papers issued to the genuine unit in Bad Reichenhall."

"There is obviously a mole in the Defense Ministry," Worden said, still holding his ground. "That does not prove I am involved."

"True," Schroeder said. "The orders could come from any of a dozen people in the ministry, but that wasn't what caught my interest. Someone had to have paid for an enormous amount of military equipment. Guns, ammunition, uniforms, trucks, radios, and the like. I wondered where all that came from."

Worden glared at him. "Anyone can buy such things on the international arms market."

"Yes," Schroeder agreed, "but who paid for it? Hauser was not a wealthy man, and none of the NOD members we've identified have that kind of capital. No, the men killed on that road yesterday had money from a wealthy, generous, sympathetic benefactor." Schroeder glanced at Braden and Rabble. "The funds to buy all that military hardware came from NATO itself, gentlemen."

Braden stared at Schroeder. "What? How the hell did that happen?" He glanced at Rabble, who, for once, looked equally dumbfounded.

Schroeder smiled. "Funds for the rally to benefit NATO had to come from NATO, of course. The original amount was just over three million euros. But about half of that money was siphoned off to an account in Zurich. The serial numbers on the rifles found at the massacre were traced to an arms dealer in Athens. He was paid from the account in Zurich."

"I have reached the end of my patience with this inane dribble," Worden said as he angrily pushed his way past Schroeder. "I am not going to stand here a moment longer. I'll find some officers to put these murderers under arrest." He stalked off toward the trailhead.

Schroeder remained where he was, but his voice rose in volume. "You, General Worden, signed the authorization for the funds to be placed in that account."

Worden had just reached the trail junction. He stopped at these words. A bead of sweat ran down his face and disappeared into his collar. "That proves nothing." His voice was not much more than a hoarse whisper.

"Molders was holding a Siemens KC2200 satellite radio in his hand. It looked familiar, but I could not remember where I had seen one like it. Then I found a way to confirm my suspicions." Schroeder turned to Braden and smiled. "In fact, it was you who gave me the opportunity."

"I did?" Braden asked, mystified.

"Yes," Schroeder said with a satisfied smile. "You wanted to search for the Romans after the battle and ask General Worden for helicopters. I took a chance and gave you Molders's radio. It was a gamble, but I had nothing to lose. You made the call, and guess who answered?" He cocked his head at Worden.

Suddenly, Braden recalled Rabble commenting on the radio that Worden had been carrying on the NATO jet. Looking at Rabble, he saw a smile on his face.

"Told you," Rabble said smugly.

Worden took a deep breath. "So says the greatest criminal investigator in all of Germany," he said, his voice dripping venom.

"Thank you for the compliment, General," Schroeder said. "I launched a full investigation into your past and associations. I made sure that all mention of who had been killed by the Romans was kept from you. I wanted you to believe the real Gebirgsjäger Battalion 232 had been massacred. That gave me all the time I needed."

The general marched back toward Schroeder, pointing a finger at him. "So that is why I was not able to reach anyone from the jet!" He clenched his teeth. "And I suppose Captain Klein was part of your little charade?"

Schroeder beamed. "Yes. Chancellor Hoffman helped me in that regard. He ordered her to do whatever Herr Braden asked. I knew you would have no choice but to follow her up here. I wanted you away from the massacre site. As long as you did not receive any calls from Hauser and Molders, you would not know what had really happened. The NOD survivors are being interrogated in Koblenz right now."

Worden's face turned the color of old cheese. "There are survivors?"

"Yes," Schroeder said, "and to use another American idiom, they are 'singing like canaries.' We will soon know everything." He put his hand on the butt of his pistol. "You never knew the Romans had done us a great favor. It is poetic justice of a sort." He slapped a mosquito on his cheek. "I'm surprised at you, Hermann. You didn't make much of an effort to conceal your tracks. Very sloppy for a professional soldier."

Morley's face showed shock and revulsion. He saw Lucius watching him and said, "Sire, that man," he pointed at Worden, "has committed a serious crime against his country."

Lucius looked at Worden. "He is a traitor?"

"Yes," Morley said. "I do not know if I can explain what has happened here. But as I understand it, that man, Hermann Worden, was trying to unify Germany and drive out all foreigners." He frowned, realizing what he had just said.

"I only want to ask you one thing," Schroeder said to the German officer. "How did you think you could get away with it?"

The general's jaw was still clenched as he spoke in a harsh voice. "If we had succeeded, there would have been no accountability. We would have had control of the government and the military. It would not matter how open our methods were. The end justified the means."

Schroeder's expression became even harder. "Hermann Worden, I am placing you under arrest for treason and conspiracy." He put the radio to his mouth. "Colonel Abel, this is Schroeder. I need two armed men to come here at once."

"I'll send them in right away," was the response over the speaker.

Worden was still talking as if he hadn't heard. "It was foolproof. We had taken every precaution. No one knew anything was happening, not NATO or the government. No one." His eyes were closed as if he were saying a prayer. "It would have worked . . . if . . . if only . . ." His cold hard eyes opened, and he looked at Lucius standing nearby. The Roman legatus stared back at him but said nothing.

"You!" Worden shouted at Lucius. "You and your dead barbarian kind destroyed a dream greater than your primitive brains could ever understand. You should never have lived. You are dead, dust to the world!" His hands were balled into fists.

Lucius remained standing where he was, his face unreadable.

Suddenly Worden advanced on him. "I'll finish you off myself, you filthy swine!"

Schroeder tried to grab the general's arm, but the taller man was too fast. He reached the body of the dead Roman and, in one quick motion, seized the sword and ran at Lucius with the weapon raised. In one savage move, he brought the gleaming blade down toward Lucius.

But the veteran Roman officer deftly sidestepped the wild slash. He drew his own sword and stabbed it into Worden's belly. Lucius said in a voice like steel, "You are not worthy to attack a Roman soldier, Arminius!"

A horrible wheezing sound escaped Worden's mouth as he tried to lift himself off the long blade buried in his body.

With a savage yank, Lucius pulled the bloody sword free, leaving the dying man to fall to the ground. A spreading pool of crimson blood soaked into the soil of the Teutoburg Forest.

It had happened in less than ten seconds. Braden and the others stared at the two men.

Lucius nodded. "I have done as I promised my long-dead friends. I have avenged all of them for the treachery of a traitor."

"Sire?" Morley said. "What do you mean?"

"My friends and comrades were killed by the treachery of a man trusted by Rome. Arminius was a traitor. I vowed to kill him myself one day. But that day was gone long before I knew it. Your Arminius has betrayed you. The death of this traitor avenges your people." He regarded the twitching man at his feet. The general was barely alive.

Lucius leaned over, looking into the fading eyes. "I respected Arminius for his motive even as I hated him for his treachery. He was acting for his people. You are below even him."

General Hermann Worden was only dead flesh on the cool forest floor.

Schroeder let out a breath and took up the radio again. "Colonel Abel, never mind."

CHAPTER XI

THE LAST LEGIONARY

The Teutoburg Forest had not changed for centuries. Birds flew and chirped among the tall trees that blocked out the sun. The ground, covered in pine needles and moss, was cool and soft underfoot.

But the world was no longer the same for a small group of people on the curve of a dirt trail, winding around the slope of a tall wooded hill.

After Schroeder left to talk to the police, Braden and the others faced the few remaining Romans. Only ten remained. Lucius talked to his legionaries, who showed no sign of fear. They were quiet as if they welcomed their inevitable fate. Then, the legatus turned to Morley. "Arthurus, our time is running out. Will you wait with us?"

Morley nodded, then turned to Sharon, standing nearby. "My dear, I want to introduce you to the last survivor of Clades Variana."

Sharon Kelly walked forward tentatively and stood in front of Lucius. "I am honored to meet you," she said in Latin. "I am Sharon Kelly."

Lucius studied her with his fathomless eyes. Sharon felt herself blushing. She realized he had probably not spoken to a woman in over two thousand years.

"I am pleased to meet you. You remind me of my beloved Livia."

"Your wife?" Sharon asked.

"Yes," Lucius said with a sad smile. "She was with the baggage train at the rear of our column when the barbarians attacked. She and my son, Cornelius, were killed." His eyes looked to the east. "I found their bodies on the road."

"I am so sorry," Sharon said, a wave of emotion sweeping through her.

Lucius shook his head. "She wanted to come on the expedition into Germania. I did not wish to leave her behind in Gallicae. If I had, she would not have been killed."

For a moment, they said nothing. The guilt the Roman felt was palpable for all. Then he sighed. "But I will soon join her. And then I may be able to assuage my guilt."

The sound of another legionary gasping for breath made them all turn. The man dropped to his knees and tried to remain upright. Then he fell, wheezing on the soft ground. Lucius went to his side. "Draconius," he said softly. "Thank you for your devoted service."

The younger man didn't hear. He was already dead.

Lucius sighed. "I am glad he was able to see his duty done," he said sadly. "We are all that is left of our once-great and powerful legion."

Morley spoke up. "Legio Fifty-four Vindicta will not be forgotten, Sire. We will tell your story to the world. I give you my word."

"Thank you, Arthurus." Then Lucius paused as if remembering something. "I have something for you." He reached into his haversack and pulled out the leather-bound codex he'd taken from the cellar. He held it out to Morley. "Gothicus Romulus was an alchemist who helped us in our quest. He wrote the entire chronicle in this journal. He gave it to me on the last day before we began the Somnum. You are a scholar, so I believe it should go to you."

Morley's sudden intake of breath betrayed how stunned he felt as he took the faded leather codex. "My God," he said hoarsely. "I . . . am truly honored."

Sharon had been examining Draconius. "Sire," she said, "may I ask you something?"

The Roman gave her a warm smile. "Yes, lovely lady. You may."

"When you went into the cellar for the last time, were the bronze lamps burning already?"

Lucius's brow rose. "Ah, no. We had been completing our labor tasks all the last day and then had a final celebration. My men were exhausted. They entered the rooms and lay down. But the wicks in the bowls were not yet alight."

"When were they lit?" Sharon asked, sensing the answer she sought was near.

Lucius thought for a moment. "After I gave my final orders to the rest of the cohort officers, we sealed the doors. We had a few candles for light. Gothicus Romulus had instructed me to set the example and light the first wick. It was on the floor beside my bunk. My friend Marcus Titus lit the one closest to him."

Braden listened to Morley's translation in awe. He saw expressions of amazement on the faces of Ann and Rabble.

"Were you the first to inhale the smoke from the bowls?" Sharon asked.

Lucius nodded. "I was."

Sharon looked about her at the other Romans. "Did any of these men also light the wicks?"

Lucius frowned. "I am not sure, but I will ask." He faced his men. "Did any of you volunteer to light the wicks of the sleeping smoke?"

All but one man raised their hands.

Sharon let out a breath. "Thank you, Sire. That was what I needed to know." She turned to Morley. "I know why they're alive, Arthur. They were the first to get the plant smoke into their systems. They inhaled the strongest, most potent doses and for the longest time."

Braden nodded. "It makes sense. They have the most in their systems. When it's completely gone, they die."

"Yes," she said. "Those who were the first to inhale the smoke lived the longest. But the others . . ." she stopped, looking at the one man who had not raised his hand.

As if on cue, he swayed on his feet and began wheezing. Another legionary gripped his arm, but he sagged to the ground and lay still.

Morley asked, "Isn't there anything we can do?"

Sharon nodded. "Yes, there is. I know how to keep them alive."

Braden asked, "How?"

"All they need to do is inhale some more smoke from the Liliacae Mallorcus plant. There is a nursery in France that sells it. We can have some sent to the University here in the city. They'll have a lab we can use." She was talking very animatedly. "I'm sure we can replicate the original method to make the paste. Once they have inhaled it, they'd go back into hibernation."

"For another two thousand years?" Rabble asked.

"No," she replied. "Under carefully controlled conditions we could bring them out of hibernation after a few months. They would continue to live."

"For how long?" Braden asked, then felt foolish. It was an absurd question. These men had outlived whole civilizations. They deserved to rest.

"I don't know," Sharon said, running her hands through her deep copper hair. "But we'd have time, time to talk to them, to learn. Maybe take them back to Rome . . ." Then she fell silent.

Lucius asked Morley what was happening.

When Morley finished, the legatus nodded slowly. He wore a thoughtful look on his face. "I see. We may be given more time? More life?"

"Possibly," Morley said.

The Roman wiped his dirty face. Then he turned to his men. "I have learned that there may be a way for us to continue living. You have always followed my commands. But this is a choice you must make for yourselves. Do any of you wish to stay alive?"

The legionaries looked at him, then talked to each other in low tones. And one by one, they all shook their heads.

Lucius nodded at their response. Then he looked directly at Sharon. "I do understand your wish to keep us alive, but that would not be doing us a service. We are tired. Our world is gone, and even returning to Rome would serve no good."

Sharon's eyes brimmed with tears. "But . . . but you can't just die! We have so much to ask you. Please . . ." She seemed almost desperate. "The things you could tell us . . ."

Morley gently placed his hand on her shoulder. "Let them go, Sharon."

She tried to fight back the tears. Then she nodded. "I'm sorry."

"I feel the same way," he said. "But you must realize what will happen to them if we did manage to extend their lifespan. They'd become objects of study like laboratory rats. And when word of their existence leaked out . . ."

She angrily wiped at the tears streaming down her cheeks. "Yes. I know just what would happen. You're right."

Jason Cannell drove the rental van down a two-lane country road at over a hundred kilometers an hour. Beside him, Moss held his GPS.

"Goddamn," Cannell swore as the electronic voice told him to turn at yet another intersection, the tenth since they'd driven out of the airport. "This is taking forever. You sure you got it programmed right?"

"It's programmed for the Kalkriese Battle Site Visitors' Center," Moss said as he grabbed his door handle in the sharp turn. The wheels screeched on the road. "It's working fine. For Christ's sake, will you slow down?"

Cannell ignored him and kept his eyes on the road ahead. After Glenn Redmond's call, Cannell contacted his boss at ENN Headquarters in Bonn and asked permission to charter a plane to take them from Wetzlar to Osnabrück. Just getting authorization had taken twenty minutes, during which Cannell had paced the hotel room like a caged tiger. At last, they climbed aboard the Dassault twin-engine jet and took off. An hour later, they landed at Osnabrück, where a rental van was waiting.

He knew his career was on the line. The charter was costing ENN over five thousand euros, and he was leaving behind one of the biggest stories of the decade. "Fuck!" he growled. "All that time lost waiting for some deskbound asshole to sign the voucher!"

"You're taking a hell of a chance," Moss said. "Dumping the massacre to chase ghosts."

"I know the big story is up here. Why else would a NATO jet and two Kraut special operations helicopters fly to a chickenshit college town like Osnabrück? There's not a military installation for two hundred klicks in any direction. That site is the only thing that seems to be connected to the massacre."

"How so?" Moss asked as the van leaned over on another curve.

"Romans, Aaron, Romans! Some lunatics dressed as Romans attacked and killed a whole shitload of German troops. And now the bigshots who were supposed to be protecting Hoffman and the rally have flown up here, to a place where a bunch of Romans got their asses kicked two thousand years ago. Does that make any sense at all?"

"No," Moss said, careful not to antagonize Cannell, who was clearly on the edge of desperation.

"Right! Things that don't make sense always have a great story behind them. I'm going to get in there, find out who is hiding at that old battlefield, and plaster their faces all over the world." The GPS gave him another direction, and he finally saw a neat sign that proclaimed, in German and English, Kalkriese Historic Battle Site.

Cannell slapped the steering wheel. "There! That's it!"

Moss shrugged. He was only the videographer. He looked out the window at the dense evergreen trees passing on either side. They hadn't seen another car on this road.

Just as the van came around another bend in the road, Cannell stomped on the brakes. "Shit!"

Moss was thrown hard against his seat belt. He always wore one when Cannell was driving. "What the hell did you do that for?" he snapped as he fell back against his seat. Then he saw two German police cars blocking the road and four armed police officers beside them. "Oh."

Cannell said, "I'll handle these Stormtroopers."

An officer dressed in neat gray trousers and a blue jacket came to the driver's side. His uniform was so perfect it looked as if it had just been pressed.

"*Guten Morgen*," he said politely. He smiled, but Moss knew the man meant business.

"*Guten Morgen*, officer," Cannell said as he pulled out his American passport and ENN credentials. I'm Jason Cannell with ENN."

The officer's smile vanished. "No one is permitted to pass," he said firmly. "This area is secured. No unauthorized persons are allowed past this post."

Cannell said, "We're here to report on the massacre at Wetzlar yesterday."

"Wetzlar is several hundred kilometers south of here," the cop said. "If you take the Autobahn south to the B21, then—"

"I know where it is," Cannell said through gritted teeth. "We just came from there."

The German's smile returned. "Then it looks as if you made the trip for nothing. There is no story here."

"I know a NATO aircraft and two helicopters landed here in the last few hours. And they were carrying people connected with the massacre."

The man remained silent.

"I'm here on the orders of ENN," Cannell said as though this was a pronouncement from God. "I have credentials from the German Ministry of Culture and Media that give me full access to any and all secured areas. You can't keep us out."

"Yes, I can," the officer said in a cold voice that sounded like something from an old war movie. "You are not permitted to enter."

Cannell felt his chance slipping away. "Look, pal, have a heart. My boss will have my head if I don't get in there. We won't be more than twenty minutes. I promise."

The cop raised one eyebrow. "Even Walter Cronkite would not be allowed in here today." He smiled. "And you are not Walter Cronkite."

Moss saw the blood rising in Cannell's face. If there was one person Jason Cannell hated to be compared to, it was Walter Cronkite. "That sanctimonious old fart was a fossilized moralistic dinosaur long before he died," the journalist had said more than once.

Cannell ground his teeth, trying not to lose his temper.

"If you persist," the German said, "I will have to take you both into custody."

"Oh, shit," Moss said almost inaudibly as he wondered if the food in German jails was any good.

"Look," Cannell started to say, but the German cut him off.

"I am not going to argue with you." The "sir" was now noticeably absent. "Turn your vehicle around and go back the way you came. Now." The last word was like the sound of breaking glass.

Cannell tried another tack. "Who is in charge here? I want to talk to your commandant."

"Colonel Abel has authority in this matter."

Cannell frowned. "Colonel? German Army?"

"No. Landespolizei."

Cannell said, "Fine. I'm going to have to talk to him. I want your name. You're making a big mistake."

The officer pulled a card from his pocket and handed it to Cannell. "You will find my name and ID number on this." Then he gave Cannell a wide smile that showed all his perfect white teeth. "By the way, we saw that story you did on the decline of the German police last year." The smile vanished. "We were not amused. Have a nice day."

Cannell watched the man return to his comrades. "Goddamned goose-stepping Nazi." He tossed the card on the floor and put the van in reverse. "Look in the glove box. Find a map of the area. GPS won't work for this. I'm getting in there one way or another, and I'm not going to let some knuckle-dragging fancy-pants Kraut public servant stop me. Hang on." He turned the van around and stomped on the accelerator.

Lucius sat against a thick log lying at the base of the steep hillside. The air was warm and fragrant with the scent of pine, moss, and sorrel. He looked at the bodies of his legionaries. They had all died in the last half an hour, and now he was the only one left.

He was having trouble breathing. His chest heaved as he gulped great lungsful of the warm air.

"Sire," said the beautiful woman with the red hair. She sat beside him on the log. "Is there anything I can do to help you?"

He showed her a warm smile. "No, lovely lady. Please do not worry." Then he saw that her hand was on his arm. It felt very warm. "You are the first woman I have talked to since I lost my wife, Livia."

Her deep green eyes flooded with tears. "I'm so sorry, Sire. You have lost so much."

He patted her hand. "I have few regrets. I have done my duty. That is enough for any soldier." He sighed.

Then the man called Alexander came to sit beside him. He seemed to want to say something, but no words came out.

Lucius looked at him. "Do not despair, my friend. This is what I wanted. I will not die in a land far from home and friends. This forest," he waved his hand at their surroundings, "has been my home and the place I most longed to return to. And now I am here, at last, among the spirits of the men I knew and loved. I am happy."

The woman nodded and wiped her face. Her other hand remained on his arm. He understood their grief and sorrow. In a way, Lucius wished he had more time to talk with them and answer their questions. But no, that was not to be. He had challenged the gods for far too long. He suddenly wondered if they still ruled the sky. Perhaps Apollo, Jupiter, Mars, and Vulcan, too, had faded into the mists of time and memory. But in the sky would certainly be waiting the men he'd known: Vitellus, Septimus, Marcus, Marius Civilus, and so many others. Perhaps even Quinctilius Varus himself. Lucius smiled as he looked around him at the tall cloak of trees and the trail winding into the dark gloom. He'd once killed many men on this very road, in this very forest. And just a short time before, he'd taken one more life. The latter-day Arminius, who had betrayed his own people. The past had come full circle.

"How poetic," he murmured. "A tale worthy of Virgilius Maro." This triggered a thought.

Reaching into the haversack, he felt the small object and drew it out. For a long moment, he regarded Livia's codex. He had read it many times since he and the few survivors had returned to Rome. Every neatly written word had been laid down by his wife's small warm hand. Her words drifted up from the ancient pages in the singsong voice he had so loved. He turned to see the old academician looking at him. "Arthurus, would you do me one favor?"

Morley nodded. "Of course," he said in a hoarse voice. "What do you wish?"

Lucius held up the codex. "Livia wrote her poems in this. No one has ever read them. They were private and personal to her. I ask, after I am dead, that you not permit anyone to read them. I wish that it be interred with me and that her words remain secret."

Morley nodded again. "I will see to it. I promise."

Lucius kissed the cover of the book and put it back in the haversack. Now only he would know his wife's thoughts.

His life was drawing to a close. He was glad he had his new friends close beside him. They alone understood.

"There," Cannell said with a note of triumph. "That's the trail." He was looking at a map of the area that Moss had found in the glove box. "I knew there'd be another way in there." The van was stopped on a narrow paved road that appeared to be for maintenance. They'd had to break open a gate to get in, but Cannell was like a man possessed. He wanted that story. With a clap on Moss's leg, he jumped from the van and pulled open the side door. "Get your gear and power it up. Get the uplink with the satellite. I don't want to lose any time when we get in there. We may only have a few minutes, and I want to get a live shot right away."

Moss did as he was told. He hoped Cannell knew what he was doing. The image of those hard-nosed German cops flitted through his mind as he retrieved his camera bag from the van. After pulling out the camera, he connected it to the satellite transmitter. In a few moments, he saw the lights blinking. "Uplink confirmed," he said.

"Great. Follow me." Without another word, the reporter trotted up the trail that led into the forest.

Moss, having no choice, followed him.

The thick branches overhead instantly blotted out the late-morning sunlight. The air temperature dropped several degrees, and Moss felt goose bumps on his bare arms. Trying to keep his footing on the rough soil of the trail, he stayed close to Cannell. The other man slowed as the trail wound between two high banks, which spouted tangles of roots like gnarled black fingers.

"I think the main road through the site is just ahead," Cannell whispered. "Keep that camera running. We may only get one chance."

Moss lifted the compact digital video camera to his shoulder and fitted his right eye into the rubber eyepiece. He kept Cannell's back in the viewfinder while keeping his other eye open to navigate on the trail. His left foot caught a thick root, and he nearly stumbled. "Shit!" Moss snarled in a whisper. "Slow down. I'm trying to walk and film at the same time."

"Quiet," his companion hissed. "I hear voices ahead. Stay here. I'm going to see if I can get closer. Keep me in sight for a wide shot. How's your light?"

"What light?" Moss grumbled to himself. "I've got you, but that's about it."

Cannell pulled a wireless microphone from his shoulder bag and switched it on. "Are you receiving my signal?"

"Got it," Moss said. In the viewfinder, he watched Cannell move hunched over as he negotiated the narrow trail. In a few more minutes, he, too, heard voices. Then Cannell's voice came through his earpiece. "Speed, Moss."

Moss didn't reply, instead focusing on the form of Cannell moving like a soldier around a clump of trees. Beyond him, the light increased as if they were emerging from the forest. The voices grew more distinct. Moss's heart raced. They were speaking English and some other language. Italian? No, something else. At least it wasn't German.

Just then, a dark shape blocked his view. Moss tried to focus on the obstruction, but before he could see what it was, a voice spoke up, loud and clear in front of him. "You are trespassing in a secured area. You will stop filming at once."

Moss lowered the camera. He knew that voice. Then the dark shape clarified itself into the hulking form of Landespolizei Commissioner Karl Schroeder. He was not smiling.

A few feet farther on, Jason Cannell was also being confronted by another police officer. But unlike Moss, Cannell wasn't about to cave in. "Commissioner Schroeder, I'm glad to see you again. I'm Jason Cannell with ENN."

"I know who you are," the officer replied curtly. "You are not permitted to be here."

"Look," Cannell began, holding up his microphone, even though Moss didn't have his camera running, "we followed that NATO jet and the two German helicopters up here. That massacre at Wetzlar is the biggest thing to happen in Germany since the war. Why have you come five hundred kilometers to an old Roman battle site? What is here to interest you? And why is the area under armed guard?"

Schroeder shrugged. "I suppose I can answer that question on the record."

Cannell shot a look at Moss, who raised his camera to focus on Schroeder.

"We arrested some of the Roman impersonators yesterday. They are members of a cult that reveres ancient Rome. After being questioned, they admitted that this site holds great significance to them. The cult held ceremonies in the forest. Apparently, they came here prior to going down to Wetzlar. The archaeologists and investigators are examining evidence that might help us identify other cult members. It's a crime scene, and we can't permit anyone to come in and spoil evidence. That's all there is to it as far as this site is concerned." Then Schroeder shrugged. "But as for the real story . . ." He checked his watch. "Chancellor Hoffman has a press conference scheduled for about ten minutes from now. He will explain what has really happened. He will also be announcing several impending indictments and arrests of certain key figures in the Defense Ministry for treason and conspiracy. All the news services will be given full access to the massacre site." He gave Cannell a sly smile. "Except for your own ENN, I believe, since you are not there to see it."

For the first time since he'd begun working with Jason Cannell, Moss wished he could have filmed the look of horror on the reporter's face.

It was nearly over. Braden watched as Lucius struggled for breath. He sat on the log next to the Roman man who had almost become a friend. He wished he could help, but there was nothing to be done. Even Sharon, who alone held the key to keeping Lucius alive, remained silent as they watched the Roman grow weaker. This man, truly the last of his kind, was braver and wiser than any man Braden had ever known. Lucius faced his death as if he welcomed it.

Then, the Roman legatus looked at him. Their eyes met. He spoke to Morley.

The archaeologist came closer. "He said he wants to give something to you, Alex."

Braden was confused. "What? I don't understand."

Lucius reached down to the belt at his waist. He pulled the ornate bronze buckle open and slid the end free. In a moment, he had pulled the belt off and wrapped it around the scabbard of his gladius. He held it out to Braden. "I want you to have this, Alexander."

Braden's eyes widened in shock. "You . . . you want me to have your gladius? Why?"

Lucius had to take a deep breath before answering. "Arthurus told me you were the only one who understood from the beginning why we rose from the cellar and marched into the land of our enemies." He placed the belt and sword in Braden's shaking hands.

"This gladius was hand-forged by an old smithy in the village where I was raised. His name was Vulcanus, and he served under Gaius Julius in Gaul. He regaled me with tales of glory and conquest. He gave me this gladius on the day I completed my training." Lucius shook his head. "Vulcanus did not live to learn of the massacre of the three legions. I have killed many times with this same blade, Alexander. Right here on this spot, during the massacre of the three legions. And today, for the last time, I have killed again. It has done its duty. I am the last legionary of the last legion. It is now yours." He faltered when the heavy sword left his hand and laid back on the cool hillside in the Teutoburg Forest.

"My loyal friends, Marcus Titus, Septimus Deo, I am coming to you at last. *Cursum perficio.*"

Then, Lucius Cassius Aquilius said no more. His breathing dropped to a whisper and finally ceased.

Braden, Morley, Sharon, Rabble, and Ann looked at him. The Teutoburg Forest suddenly grew still and silent. No one spoke.

Lucius's face was dirty, unshaven, the eyes closed under the brow of his helmet. But he was smiling. The Roman had at last found peace.

"It began here two thousand years ago," Morley said in a whisper. "And as he just said, 'here my journey has ended.'"

Holding the ancient sword in his shaking hand, Braden heaved a long sigh. "No, it does not end here. Legio Fifty-four will be remembered." He pointed at the codex Morley was holding. "That book will change history."

The older man nodded as he ran his fingers over the worn and cracked leather binding. "I'll make sure of it."

"That will be their true legacy." With one last look at Lucius, Braden hugged Ann close and turned to walk out of the Teutoburg Forest.

ACKNOWLEDGMENTS

This book has undergone scores of rewrites and edits over a period of ten years. It bears little resemblance to the original version, which ran to about 150,000 words. Now it is a four-part series totaling more than a quarter of a million words. It still amazes me that I wrote this book. But I did not do it myself. Yes, I did the writing, the research, and the endless rewrites, but I was only the spearpoint of a large team of wonderful people who aided, encouraged, and even drove me to keep going and finish the damn book.

Authors of written works rarely take full credit for their accomplishments, at least the honest ones. I am glad and honored to acknowledge the contributions of so many people. A bit of background will help. I am blind and have been so for nearly twenty years, long before I began this book. But I was already a historian, writer, and aspiring bestselling author, the latter still in the future. I work and write with a complex array of technology and tools that make it possible for me to live and work with confidence.

But thanks to these tools, I was only faced with the same challenges that any sighted writer deals with—that of coming up with a story and putting it on paper. That was the hard part, not being blind. In any event, being a blind writer has few serious obstacles other than those we all face in the ever-changing world of computers and software. I am extremely grateful to my longtime friend Don Ramm, a former Air Force pilot, who, for some reason that still baffles me, has spent hundreds of hours to keep my computers and hardware working. I depend on my internet connections, email, and network to do my job. If Don had not been there for me, I'd have to write my books like Fred Flintstone, with a slate and chisel, or with Windows Vista, which would be even worse. My email would be smoke signals and my phone a pair of tin cans and a string. Don, you are a true and devoted friend. I could never earn enough in royalties to repay you for all your work. I am truly grateful. May the wind always be under your wings.

I am glad to offer my gratitude to my good friend Linda Stull, who gave so much of her time and effort to seeing my dreams come true. Every book and nearly every article I have written went under her careful, patient, and precise scrutiny. She read every word, and even though we often disagreed on certain points, we now agree that this is a far better book as a result.

My parents Eric and Margit Carlson gave me a love of history and reading but did not live to see my first book published. But I think of them with every book I write, hoping they know that I am carrying on the legacy they left me. My cousin, Katerina Petersson, was a fan of my writing and encouraged me to keep it up. Like my mother, she instilled a love of reading and history that opened the world of the past to my hungry mind and imagination.

My older brother David and I shared a love of history and reading, and he was an excellent sounding board for ideas and suggestions.

My buddy Rob Wood and his sweet wife, Elaine, spent a great deal of time helping me move forward after Jane's death. I can never express enough gratitude to them for all they have done. My friends John and Anita Campbell, neighbors Carol Gendel, Kate Rogelstad Janelle Personius, John and Geneva Tolbert, John and Mary Lou Rushing, Gigi Harrington, Kimmy Aguinaldo, and other residents of Madrid Manor were the Earthbound angels in my life.

My brothers and sisters at Hope United Methodist Church, like the warm and caring people they are, gave so much to help me move forward and not give up. John and Linda Missoni, Vince and Lynn Cramer, Pastor Brian Kent, Paul Swaykowski, and the members of the Thursday Knights Bible Study group were always there when I needed them. I have never known such comfort and contentment from any group of people in my life. May God bless them all.

Back when I was first considering this book, I became involved with a Roman Legion reenactment group in San Diego. Legio IX Hispaña was run by a colorful and only slightly mad Irishman named Sean Richards. I learned a lot about the life of a Roman legionary from the men of Legio IX. My closest friend in the legion was Optio Mario Padillo. Tall, strong, and handsome with dark wavy hair and chiseled features, Mario looks like Central Casting's idea of a Roman centurion. He helped me understand what it was like for the legionaries of the first century. From the start he was enthusiastic about this book project, even going so far as to urge me to get it published in 2009, the two thousandth anniversary of the Varian Disaster. But since I had not yet even started the manuscript, and this was in 2008, that was unlikely.

For three years I was a member of the prestigious Rancho Bernardo Writers' Group, headed by Peter Berkos, an avuncular and supportive leader. He and the other members of the RBWG read my manuscript and provided excellent (although not always heeded) advice. They helped make this book far better than it was. Maryjane Roe, Mo Kindle, Terry Ambrose, Manjula Panday, and the others are all writers and authors. I very much hope to see their books alongside mine in bookstores.

My relationships with the Pearl Harbor Survivors Association, Distinguished Flying Cross Society, Order of Daedelians, American Ex-POWs, Commemorative Air Force, San Diego Air & Space Museum, and many other organizations have enriched my life and provided a wealth of articles, interviews, and friendships. I am proud to be friends with many members of the Navy, Army, Marine Corps, other veterans, and NASA astronauts. More than a few were World War II, Korean War, and Vietnam War veterans. While none had any direct connection with the armies of the Roman Empire, they often provided a keen insight into the mind of the soldier. For these people, who have been my biggest fans and supporters, I give my everlasting gratitude.

For the greater glory of Rome!

Mark Carlson
Augustus MMXXII

ABOUT THE AUTHOR

MARK CARLSON, a resident of San Diego, has been a lifelong student of military history. Legally blind, he works with advanced software on his computer and travels with a Guide Dog. He has never considered his blindness to be an obstacle, only a challenge.

For the past twenty years Carlson has been a regular contributor to more than a dozen military history publications. In that time, he has written over two hundred articles and interviewed hundreds of veterans, actors, historians, and authors. A former Civil War and Roman re-enactor, Carlson has gained an insight into the world of the fighting man to bring depth and realism into his writing. He is very passionate about history, considering it an obligation to remember the past with respect.

His first non-fiction book published by Sunbury Press, *The Marines Lost Squadron: The Odyssey of VMF-422*, was highly acclaimed by respected military historians.

His magazine articles run the gamut of topics from aviation, naval, and military history, classic film and television, dogs, humor and essays. He started by writing stories about his first Guide Dog, Musket, and later, about his work at the San Diego Air & Space Museum.

A former president of a San Diego Toastmasters club, he tours the country doing lectures on history for colleges and adult education programs. A popular speaker for several national military museums and groups, he is a member of several veteran and historical organizations.

Printed in Great Britain
by Amazon